A Natural Passion

Tammy Mannersly

A Natural Passion
Copyright © 2021 Tammy Mannersly
All rights reserved.

ISBN (ebook) 978-1-953335-63-0
(print) 978-1-953335-64-7

Inkspell Publishing
207 Moonglow Circle #101
Murrells Inlet, SC 29576

Cover art By The Write Designer

OTHER BOOKS BY TAMMY MANNERSLY

TAMMY MANNERSLY

DEDICATION

For those who appreciate the simple pleasures in life and who value all of nature's creatures.

TAMMY MANNERSLY

CHAPTER ONE

Wandering carefully through the spinifex-strewn sand dunes of Mon Repos beach, Dylan O'Day used a specially designed, turtle-safe flashlight to guide his way on the unmarked track. The calming roar of the Pacific Ocean, the curling waves colliding with the golden sand, provided a soundtrack to his usual early morning patrol.

He'd come to the Mon Repos Turtle Center, just north-east of Bundaberg along the Queensland coast, at half past three in the morning as he had most days for the past eight years. As a part-time park ranger and a marine biologist for the Merchant Marine Science Center located just down the road, Dylan had spent most of his time concerned with researching and protecting the large number of marine turtles which frequented the globally significant site. That was until *she* arrived.

He was supposed to be her mentor, he reminded himself for the umpteen time.

Yet, it didn't seem to stop him from thinking about her. Her sweet smile, her astute hazel eyes, her passion for aquatic wildlife, which one of the numerous things they had in common.

She'd been the successful applicant of a paid internship,

a six-month hands-on course offered by his employer, Max Merchant, to help students interested in marine studies gain practical experience. She was off limits – until the internship concluded.

"You're ten years her senior," Dylan scolded himself in hushed tones.

What drew him to her? What made her so alluring? There were plenty of kind, attractive women his own age he could date. Though none were as passionate about the ocean and protecting the sealife as she was. Most of them didn't understand his work, they didn't care for the odd hours he kept or his strange routines which were necessary to help protect both turtles and hatchlings alike. *She* did.

As Dylan continued his patrol higher into the sand dunes, a change in the familiar landscape drew his attention away from his conflicted thoughts. The sand around a flagged turtle nest had been disrupted. A tug of worry pulled at his gut. They couldn't have lost another one, could they? It would be the second this month.

Shining his flashlight over the spot, he saw a well had been dug by something or someone and the eggs were gone – or eaten.

He bent down beside it, pulling at the sides of his khaki cargo pants to make the movement easier. Reaching into the empty nest, he brushed at the sand with his fingers, looking for traces of shell, a sign of predator attack, but he found none. The eggs, whole and intact, had been taken.

Anger boiled within him. His hand shook as he unclipped the radio transceiver from his belt. Dylan stood, lifting it to his lips and pressed the button on the side.

"Attention base," he said, doing his best not to sound gruff.

There was a crackle of static as he removed his finger from the button and waited.

"Base here." Brian's croaky voice sounded tinny through the device.

Dylan was relieved it was Thursday and the elderly man

was on duty. While other staff might have been distracted or sleep-deprived due to the early hours, Brian had adjusted to the unusual schedule and was always enthusiastic on the line.

"Dylan here."

"Go for Dylan."

"I think we've been hit by poachers again."

"Again." The older man parroted back. His voice in shock.

"A flagged nest high on the dunes. Number twelve."

"Noted," Brian said glumly. "Geez, Dylan. We'd counted one hundred and thirty at that site. The clutch of eggs looked healthy. We'd hoped it would be one of the most successful."

"You don't have to remind me," Dylan replied, his tone taut but matter-of-fact. "We have to catch those bastards, Bri. The ecosystem will suffer if we keep losing eggs at this rate."

"Too right."

"I'm going to continue on patrol, see if I notice any other problems or things out of the ordinary."

"Careful, Dylan. Who knows if those guys are still around."

"Sure thing. See you in an hour for breakfast. Over."

"I'll get Sandra to make it a hot one. See you at six. Over and out."

A smile tugged at Dylan's lips as he clipped the radio back onto his belt.

The Australian summer began last month, keeping the weather hot and humid. Even with the warm days, a hearty breakfast of eggs and bacon was worth looking forward to after a long patrol.

The coming sunrise lightened the sky and turned the midnight blues of night above the crashing waves into calm mauves. The line of the horizon began to burn with a warm, orange glow. Continuing further along the sand dune, Dylan pushed aside his anger and need for retribution, stirred up by the ransacked nest. Instead of devising ways to harm the poachers if he ever found them, Dylan started another mental list of why *she* remained off limits to him. At the top sat the fact he had more important things to focus his attention on – they both did. Romantic flings—no matter how much he wanted her—didn't make the grade when there was illegal poaching going on.

But, what if…

The damned optimist in him wouldn't give up, always going on about 'what if'. He couldn't have her, he shouldn't have her, and knew better than to hope for the impossible.

The problem was it wasn't impossible. He knew she liked him, maybe not quite in that way – yet, but there was hope. Too bad he couldn't stop wishing for more. Maybe her feelings could grow, even become love as he loved her – his passionate *Kyra*.

*

It wasn't really wrong, was it? Technically she wasn't spying on him, he just happened to be in her line of sight. Yeah, that was it.

Kyra Shine sat at the computer, going over the estimated predictions for the hatchlings this season as she'd been asked. Was it her fault the desk she was using happened to be on the second story of the Merchant Marine Science Center and also in front of the large picture window which overlooked the sparse, green yard out back? How was she to know he'd planned to hose down the boats, shirtless, even though he did it most mornings after the crew had gathered their daily samples and statistics from along the coast? Maybe this would be the day he wouldn't? He was and boy, she thoroughly enjoyed watching him.

His lean, muscular body was bronzed. It glistened with

the spray of the water under the midday sun. Somehow, he'd managed to get himself entirely wet. Even the small, navy shorts which ensured him some modesty were slicked tight to his body from the moisture. He waved the nozzle of the hose in front of the silver hull of the small motor boat. His biceps contorting and bulging with the movement, making Kyra wonder what it would feel like to have those arms wrapped around her. She shivered at the thought and then mentally kicked herself for it.

Could she be any more of a lovesick girly-girl? She was nearly twenty-two after all, well into grownup-hood, if there was such a term, and well beyond schoolgirl crushes and yet, that's exactly how she felt around him. He gave her butterflies in the stomach, made her all giggly, naïve and stupid. She knew he wasn't perfect. He had a dangerous streak of bad-boy, but it didn't matter to her. She was smitten.

He turned his head and slicked his wet, light-brown hair back with his free hand as he glanced upward. His triangular jaw lifted as he glanced toward the window. The surprise of his brown eyes meeting hers through the glass of the window had her flinching. Her hand flapped to the side and knocked over the canister of pens on the desk, scattering them across the desktop. Kyra snapped her eyes to the mess she'd made and ducked her head to hide the fact she'd been caught staring at him. With her heart racing, she hurried to tidy the clutter before anyone else walked in.

"Did you see a spider?"

The familiar masculine voice with its deep, velvety tones had her spinning around so fast in her swivel chair she almost toppled over.

"Whoa! Didn't mean to frighten you."

He was at her side, helping to steady her. His strong, warm hand was firm on her bare shoulder.

"Thanks, Dylan," Kyra said and risked a glance up at her mentor's handsome face. "I just…I wasn't expecting you back so soon."

She ran a hand through her lopsided, strawberry blonde bob, then tried to straighten her scarlet singlet before offering him a small smile. He beamed at her, his perfect grin brightening his face, reaching his blue-green eyes, making them glitter. Grabbing the chair at the desk beside hers, he took a seat and then shrugged.

"I got tired of repeating myself to the police. I'm not sure what more I could say. I found the nest empty, with no clear sign of the culprit." Dylan scratched absent-mindedly at the shadow of auburn beard on his square jaw. "Without more information to go on, they're handicapped. They offered to have a car patrol the coastal roads throughout the night in case the poachers are getting in and out by vehicle and they've suggested we start organizing our own rostered patrols in groups of two or more just to be on the safe side."

Kyra remained a little flustered by her friend's sudden arrival. Had he seen her? She hoped not.

She nodded. Her thoughts returned to the memory of the theft, causing a churning in her gut. "Good idea. I really hope the police can catch those douchebags before another nest is destroyed."

Dylan watched her carefully, his head tilting, making his thick, tousled mop of auburn hair sway slightly with the movement. Even though he was seated, he presented an imposing figure in his black jeans and grey T-shirt. He was a very tall man, nearing six-foot-five and his bulky, muscular physique reminded her of a wild, mountain man she'd seen on TV. Although big and burly, Dylan was a gentle soul, kind and compassionate. She trusted him whole-heartedly, but couldn't tell him about...her infatuation.

She knew he wouldn't laugh at her, but it was sure to be awkward. Even with her crush on someone else, there was something sincere and intense between them. Whatever it was, she didn't want it affected. Friend or something more…she cared about Dylan too much to risk losing him. Besides until she understood her own mind, she'd keep her feelings to herself.

Concern filled his blue-green eyes as his hand returned to her shoulder for a moment. He patted the tanned skin of her arm, sending shivers down her spine.

"You okay?"

"Sure." She heard the nervous lilt in her voice and felt the jitteriness in her slender limbs before her gaze twitched toward the window.

Kyra pursed her lips, then tried for another smile as she forced her gaze back to his, but it was too late. Dylan looked out the window, the attractive features of his face contorting in annoyance.

"Looks like the boss's son is at it again."

Her pulse twitched at the gruffness in his tone. Had he realized her secret? She glanced at Dylan quickly then followed his line of sight.

Jake Merchant – son of Max Merchant, the owner and founder of the Merchant Marine Science Center – was still wet and shirtless as he offered the lithe blonde next to him a flirtatious smile.

"Who's that?" Kyra fought the urge to rub a hand over her injured heart.

Dylan grimaced, then shook his head in obvious criticism. "One of the postgraduate students from James Cook University in Townsville. They're visiting for the day, gathering their own samples to take back."

He huffed as Kyra nibbled on her lower lip, their eyes still fixed to the scene below.

"He'd better be on his best behavior or his father will have his hide," Dylan growled. "He's already on thin ice. One final step away from losing this job and his cushy accommodation on the grounds." Dylan's face softened, as his gaze returned to hers. "Nothing for you to worry about, Kyra. Jake's always pushing the boundaries. It's just a shame he doesn't appreciate the opportunity Max has given him."

Kyra nodded automatically, but felt the need to challenge Dylan's criticism. "I'm sure he does."

Although she was new to the small team, having only started her internship four months ago, she truly felt that Jake, of all people, was someone she understood on a deeper level. She'd accepted that he had a little *bad guy* in his blood, but he'd often told her how enthusiastic he was about the work and the research they were doing.

"You forget," Dylan reminded her, "I've known him ever since I was head-hunted for the senior marine biologist position eight years ago. In all this time, I waited for him to grow up, but he never has."

Dylan's jovial smirk pulled at something in Kyra's heart and had her returning the expression, even though she felt she should've been insulted on Jake's behalf.

"Is that why Max is making you a legal partner in the business?" She did her best to sound nonchalant. "He thinks you'll be a better successor than his son?"

As his dark auburn eyebrows furrowed, Dylan chuckled sharply with surprise. "Where did you hear that?" He shook his head, dismissing the question with a wave of his hand. "Don't bother. I know the walls have ears." He shrugged modestly. "I guess. Really, I think it has more to do with priorities. Max and I, we care about conservation, protecting wildlife and their ecosystems. Jake, on the other hand… cares only about himself."

Kyra frowned, she couldn't exactly argue with that. Jake could be – at times – a little self-involved. She'd guessed he'd been spoilt as a child, at least until his teens when his mother had passed away. But maybe being overlooked to inherit the business had contributed to his acting out?

"Seriously, Kyra," Dylan said as he stood and rested that strong, supportive hand on her shoulder again. "There's no need for you to worry. Max is good at smoothing any feathers that Jake ruffles. Everything will be fine." The corners of his lips quirked upward and the concern on his face morphed into something more joyful. "I know what will cheer you up. Max suggested we all go out for a day trip to Lady Musgrave Island again tomorrow. See if we can get some visual stats on the turtles out there."

His news made her smile. She narrowed her eyes at him playfully. "Do I get a turn steering the catamaran?"

It was a job often reserved for Dylan or Max, but she enjoyed it immensely. If she couldn't bargain for it now, she didn't know when she'd get a better time.

He smirked at her, obviously impressed by her sudden change of emotion. "I'm sure we can work something out."

TAMMY MANNERSLY

CHAPTER TWO

Brightly-colored butterflyfish flittered in and out of the chunky volcanic rock as Kyra swam closer through the calm water of the Basin. The sheltered, man-made swimming area just down the coast from Mon Repos in the town of Bargara was a popular destination for families to interact with the glorious specimens of sealife without the dangers of rough water or sharks. Kyra enjoyed her weekends here, since arriving in the small community.

After Dylan had discovered a second clutch of eggs had been stolen, fear and anger rumbled through her and unsettled her stomach. Feeling on edge not knowing if those baby turtles were going to make it, she'd wanted a distraction to quiet her thoughts and pacify her emotions. She'd desperately needed the Basin today and the therapy it offered her soul.

Unlike the skittish, iridescent damselfish that kept close to the safety of the thick, black rocks, the curious butterflyfish snuck out from crevices as though trying to discover if Kyra was there to feed them like many of the tourists who dropped in for a dip. While she wasn't one of those extra friendly visitors who offered them bread or other tidbits – believing instead that the fish should inevitably find their own source of natural food in their surroundings – she was still able to admire the stunning creatures up close as they glided through the water in front of her. The underwater world was incredible. Life there seemed so vibrant, just magical.

Back home in Hervey Bay, about an hour and a half south-east of Bundaberg, she would often spend her free time at the beach, snorkeling or swimming, or just enjoying the sun, the sand and the water. There was something about the wide-open space of the ocean. It called to her, rejuvenated her, and made her feel free. The thought of being stuck inland was a nightmare. It was one of the reasons she'd decided to complete her Bachelor of Animal Ecology at the University of the Sunshine Coast in her hometown, so she could always remain close to the water.

Needing air, Kyra rose to the surface, blowing through the mouthpiece of her snorkel to clear the tube of water. Freeing it from her lips, the snorkel hung to the side of her jaw as she lifted the underwater mask from her eyes to rest atop her head. She breathed deeply, sucking in fresh air before licking the saltiness of the sea water from her lips. Her hands sculled the water easily, side to side, as she punched her slender legs, treading water slowly to keep herself afloat during high tide.

She could see the beach, see the colorful children's playground in the surrounding parkland to her right and the choppy waves hitting the long sandy shore of Kelly's Beach to her left. It was a unique perspective, seeing the world from out in the water. She felt like a mermaid spying on the life of the land-folk. Kyra saw kids building sandcastles with their parents, women sunbathing in bikinis on vibrantly colored towels and a group of boys kicking around a soccer ball.

She noticed a familiar figure. He came from Kelly's Beach and headed toward the Basin. Dark green shorts hung to his knees and a yellow towel lay wrapped around his neck, covering nearly half of the muscular physique she'd spent many hours daydreaming about. Before she could stop herself, she'd paddled closer to shore, pulling herself forward with the smooth, sliding strokes of a strong breaststroker. She was on her feet in the shallows by the time he reached the Basin's foreshore.

"Jake." She waved a hand as she stepped free of the water and onto the dry sand.

He turned to look at her, his features harsh as though contorted with frustration. Kyra realized she still had the snorkel gear plastered to her head.

Feeling the heat of embarrassment flush her cheeks, she yanked the plastic mask with its connected tube from her forehead and ran her free hand through the damp mass of her strawberry blonde bob to flatten any unruly strands.

His expression warmed as he watched her, a smile pulling at his lips as he changed direction and headed toward her.

"What are you up to, Shine? Playing with the fishes?"

"Something like that," she agreed, fighting back the girlish giggle that wanted to burst from her lips as soon as those gorgeous brown eyes had met hers.

His gaze dropped and roamed over her body for a moment. His head nodded slightly with the movement. Kyra's nipples hardened under his stare, and the heated tingling of desire clawed at her. Warmth blossomed over her skin. She glanced down, checking that her body was still hidden beneath the flimsy material of the red and white frangipani bikini.

"Lucky fishes," he drawled, dragging his gaze back to hers.

She chuckled, suddenly tense. "You've seen me in this bikini before, Jake. It's nothing special."

"Nothing special." He stepped forward, closing the gap between them. "I would never say that."

His fingers reached up, skimming her collarbone before

slipping under the thin rope of material that formed the halter around her neck. He slid them along her skin, the hot, rough, dryness of him against the soft, moistness of her. They caressed their way up to her neck and then back down, just above the cup of the bikini's bra. He let his fingers linger there, his chocolate brown eyes gazing deep into her own.

Jake stepped back from her reluctantly. "What are you doing tomorrow night?"

Her dark blonde brows narrowed as she tried to calm her ragged breathing. "Sunday?"

He nodded.

"That's family night," Kyra began again. "I mean, you know we can't miss family night. Your dad always invites everyone from the Turtle Center and the Science Center for a big barbeque. Everyone who wants to come is invited."

He shrugged. "Maybe we don't want to come this time?"

She giggled. "And, what are we going to do instead?"

Jake reached for her free hand, holding it, cool and damp against the warmth of his. "Go out for dinner. Somewhere nice. Together."

Her heart palpitated a quick rhythmic jig at the prospect of some intimate alone time together.

"Are you sure?"

He gave her a sexy smirk. "Well, we could skip dinner altogether."

Kyra was certain her heart actually stopped for a second while a lustful ache shot through her limbs. Something carnal deep within her growled, while a girly giggle passed her lips. Mortified, she cut it short and cleared her throat. "Let's just start with dinner and see where things go from there."

Jake grinned. "Sounds good."

He took a step back, releasing her hand. As he turned to leave, Kyra reached for him. Her hand met the taut muscle of his forearm and she glanced up. Her five-foot-eight frame required her to tilt her head back to look up into his eyes.

"Watch it, Shine, you know I'm not into clingy girls," he teased.

"Yes." She shook her head. "I mean, no." Kyra chuckled nervously again and released his arm, holding her hands up in surrender. "Not clingy. I just wanted to ask you something."

He seemed pleased, smug almost and for some reason that still made her feel gooey inside.

"Ask what?"

She bit her lower lip. "Why now?" She lowered her hand and fiddled with the snorkeling gear. "Why are you asking me out now? I don't mean to ruin my chances. I'm just curious. I've been here for four months. What made you decide to ask now?"

Jake frowned, looking somewhat perplexed before his face brightened again. "Would you believe money? My father finally increased my allowance. It sounds pathetic being that I'm twenty-four and allowances should be a thing of the past, but he pays me a pittance to work at the Center. The extra money means I can actually have a life and start doing more things, like taking you out." He grinned at her. "I wanted our first date to be somewhere nice."

Kyra's heart swelled and she felt all fuzzy inside. He'd waited so he could please her. It was more romantic than she'd thought possible from him.

"That is the sweetest thing," she told him. "But you didn't have to. I would've been happy having a cheap picnic of fish and chips."

His grin faltered slightly. "What? Like on the grass with the ants?"

She shrugged wistfully. "Or on the sand. Really, Jake, I'm pretty easily pleased."

His smug, smile returned. "That's what I was counting

on."

Kyra laughed at his teasing and set him free with a friendly wave of her hand.

*

Dylan sighed loudly and rubbed his eyelids with his fingertips. He'd put in a long day, one which had turned into a long night. Now the glow of the computer screen had begun to get to him. It probably hadn't helped that he hadn't switched on any lights in the large workroom after the sun set. At the time, leaving the research for his article on loggerhead turtles to brighten his environment hadn't seemed as important. Besides, the security lights on the wide porches would guide him safely downstairs or in tonight's case, to the spare room.

Max had created the Merchant Marine Science Center from two refurbished, double-story Queenslander-style homes linked together by paths and wooden platforms. While one of the spacious, timber buildings comprised the staff quarters, bathrooms and a communal kitchen. The other was where Max and Dylan kept their offices and where all the science happened. It created a terrific base of operations, providing something many organizations lacked – housing for regular staff as well as for visiting national and international specialists and aficionados. It meant the Center was regularly frequented by some of the most prominent experts in the field and the research there was always world-leading.

Dylan saved his article, backing it up on the external hard drive, before shutting down the computer. He looked at the glowing hands on the dial of his wristwatch. It was just after ten. While his home was only up Mon Repos Road a little way and down Harmony Avenue, he often found it more convenient to sleep on base. Besides, if he couldn't rest, he could jump back on the computer or head into the lab.

He knew Max, who lived in the converted apartment above the site's enormous garage, thought he was a fixture here, but neither of them seemed to mind. Max had even suggested for Dylan to keep the key to the spare room and make it his own. But Dylan hadn't taken the more permanent leap.

After locking the workroom door, he strode along the wooden slats of the porch then crossed the platform that linked the second stories of both buildings together. His footsteps were silent against the constant chirping of the cheerful crickets in the bushland around the property. It was pleasing to hear the noises of the night and know the insect life was happy. It was only when it was silent, they had reason to be concerned.

When he reached the other side, he went to the first door and unlocked it. His bag from the night before still lay on the bed. Luckily, he'd stuffed a few extra shirts inside on the off chance he'd decided to crash again, but the blue jeans he'd put on that morning would have to last another day. He started to unbutton his checkered shirt, but thought better of it. Snatching the little leather case which held his toiletries, he headed back out the door and to the communal bathroom in the middle of that level.

He made his way down the corridor to a comfortable changing space, complete with wooden benches, wall racks with coat hooks, and a line of washbasins below a wide, wall-length mirror. He took out his toothbrush, squeezed some paste on the end and began brushing his teeth at a basin. He could hear the sound of someone showering, but he couldn't quite distinguish where the sound was coming from. Using the mirror, Dylan glanced toward the two short corridors at each end of the room, noting the familiar picture of a mermaid on one and a merman on the other. The space in-between held two larger lockable rooms, one marked as a unisex bathroom, the other handicapped shower and toilet facilities. To ensure his staff and guests were happy, Max had had both floors fitted with identical facilities, which were accessible by internal and external stairs and ramps.

As he rinsed his mouth, cleaned and dried the toothbrush, the sound of showering water stopped. He knew it was likely to be Jake, having come home from a night out partying. Even though Jake's room was on the lower level, he often ventured upstairs whenever the mood took him. Or it could possibly be Heinrich, the biological oceanographer visiting from the German Marine Research Consortium whose room was next to the spare. Or maybe it was Kyra. Her room was only at the other end of the second floor. That thought had him lingering, even after he'd washed his face, using a hand-towel from the supplied pile to pat his face dry.

Dylan's heart skipped a beat, his breath catching as the sound of bare feet slapping against tiles seemed to near. He glanced up, looking through the mirror at the brightly lit corridor with the small image of a mermaid, hopeful that his preference might be correct. The footsteps grew louder and then there was a gruff, scoffing sound.

"It's only you, O'Day," Jake sneered with disappointment. "I thought I might have been lucky."

Dylan's gaze shot to the other side of the room, noting the half-naked playboy, before he turned to face him. "Sorry to disappoint you, Jake." He didn't bother to hide the sarcasm.

Jake's grin was reptilian as he approached the washbasin, his bare chest and ash-brown hair still glistened from the shower. He was shorter than Dylan, leaner where he was bulky, and sinewy where Dylan was strong, but he was younger by nearly a decade, something Dylan couldn't compete with when it came to Kyra.

"No bother." Jake leaned his towel-covered hip on the edge of the porcelain and crossed his arms over his hairless chest. "I've got a date tomorrow night. I'm bound to get lucky then."

Disdain creased his face. "Tomorrow's Sunday, that's

family night. You know your father prefers you to attend."

Jake laughed haughtily. "Team bonding and all, it's not really my scene. Besides, Kyra jumped at the opportunity to pike out. We're going to Kacy's instead."

An icy chill gripped Dylan's heart and his limbs turned to lead. *Jake and Kyra were going out to a restaurant, on a date?* His throat went dry. Maybe Kyra had found some good qualities in Jake that Dylan had missed? Some admirable characteristics he shared with his father? If that were true, then why did Dylan feel such a strong compulsion to protect her from him?

Jake spat out another condescending laugh. "What's up, old man? You can't possibly be surprised she wants a piece of this," he gestured to his chiseled abdominal muscles and then shrugged proudly. "A lot of ladies do."

Dylan gritted his teeth until it hurt his jaw. *He couldn't punch him, could he?* Maybe Max would forgive him. Clenching one fist at his side, Dylan reached out and grasped his leather toiletries case.

"You better look after her, Jake," Dylan bit the words out. "She's only an intern here. We're the ones in power, so we have to protect her."

Jake made a harsh scoffing sound in the back of his throat. "I'm not her parent. She's a big girl. She can make her own decisions. It's not my fault if she gets hurt and it's not like there are any rules against staff and interns dating."

No, just common decency and good morals. "Just use your head." Dylan nearly pleaded, though he was sure it wouldn't do any good. "Don't do anything stupid and if she says *no*, she means it."

Jake's sneery smile was full of irritation and ferocity, but Dylan ignored it and turned his back on him to leave.

"You must think I'm a real loser," Jake called after him.

Dylan shook his head slightly, refusing to turn around as he continued to stride away. *Loser* wasn't exactly the right description, his would've included more expletives.

He raised a hand above his shoulder to wave a curt goodbye. "Night, Jake."

There was a muffled growl behind him, something along the lines of '*I'll show you*', but Dylan was too tired to wait for Jake to show him anything.

CHAPTER THREE

"Come on, Shine. Stay for another drink. It's still early."

Kyra stood with her hand on the door handle of Jake's car as she waited for him to unlock it. His hand was in her other one, his grip firm, not quite pulling. She looked back at him and laughed cheerfully.

They'd just left the waterfront restaurant in Bargara after a delicious meal and a somewhat romantic evening together. Now they dawdled in the carpark adjacent to the beachfront. Much to her surprise, Jake had kept things friendly and sweet. His gentlemanly manners were in full force, pulling her chair out and holding her hand. She'd expected to be nearing second base by dessert and yet, here they were, still holding hands, and waiting on their first kiss.

She was tempted to accept his offer and see where that led them, but she'd promised Max she'd drop in to the barbeque before it ended. Besides, she wasn't really a sleep-with-the-guy-on-the-first-date kind of girl – even for someone as gorgeous as Jake.

Kyra was undeniably attracted to him, both in looks and personality, but still she felt hesitant. Was she waiting for something? A sign? Or for him to prove how he really felt? She wouldn't shy away from a kiss if it was offered, but anything below the waist would have to wait. Second dates were always better anyway, and even though he hadn't yet popped the question for one, she was sure it was coming.

"I can't," she pleaded playfully with him. "I promised I'd stop by."

He frowned at her like an irritated child on the verge of a tantrum and she laughed again.

"Don't be like that." She crooned in a soothing tone. "We can drop in to say hi, grab a couple of beers, then head out the back and sit under the stars."

Jake's lower lip poked out in a childish pout. "Yeah, with the bugs."

Kyra narrowed her eyes, her lips twitching in a teasing smirk. "I thought you were a man of the wilderness, isn't that what you're always telling me? You love all animals, even the incy-wincy ones."

He smiled and stepped closer, slipping a comforting arm around her shoulders. "Sure, I love them all – as long as they respect my space. I live inside. The creepy crawlies stay outside."

She cuddled closer to him and laughed. "A man after my own heart."

Jake slipped his hand into the back pocket of his jeans. His black sedan beeped, its lights flashing in response to the unlocking signal from the car key.

"Okay, fine." Jake conceded. "You've convinced me. I'll take you back."

He stepped away, his arm slipping from her shoulders just enough for his free hand to reach hers on the car door handle. As his dark brown eyes gazed down into hers, he lifted the handle and tugged the door open slightly.

"Thank you," she murmured, captivated by his gaze and the warmth of his body against hers.

She waited. She didn't want to be the one to make the

first move, but he was there, so close to her. Kyra was frightened this might be her only opportunity. She couldn't bear to miss out.

Her full lips pressed against his before her heart could thump out another beat. His mouth was sweet, like the caramel from their dessert mixed with the rum from his drink. She tasted him as his arms wrapped around her. His hands skimmed over the emerald-lace of her short-sleeved blouse down to the tight black material of her pants. Her hands followed suit, sliding over the soft fabric of his black shirt before slipping around his neck.

His tongue was persistent, demanding entrance into her mouth before she was ready to let go of savoring the sweetness of his lips. But she let him in to explore, let his tongue caress hers as their mouths continued their passionate dance.

Jake pulled away suddenly. His hands still clung to the curves of her body.

"Wow, Shine," he panted, "that was…"

As his voice trailed off, Kyra knew she could finish his sentence for him. It was *delicious. Satisfying* even. Maybe even *addictive*, but…

There shouldn't have been any buts…but, had it felt quite right?

She smiled sweetly up at him. "I guess we should go do our duty?"

"What?" Jake frowned down at her for a moment as though processing, his gaze still partially starry-eyed, before he nodded in understanding. "Right. Let's head back."

He held the door for her, continuing on the gentlemanly streak and she climbed in.

*

"You're not coming in?"

Dylan heard the surprise in Kyra's voice even over the

bubbly pop music thumping. He and many of the other attendees outside the Merchant Marine Science Center glanced over at the black Holden Commodore in the long drive. Even in the dim glow of the fairy lights, Dylan knew it was Jake's car. It was as perfectly detailed as its owner. He couldn't understand why Jake would enter the compound with the music blaring, so everyone would notice and then refuse to join the gathering?

Kyra slammed the passenger-side door, her beautiful face contorted in agitation and then perplexity. Dylan glanced at Max. His gracious boss was already making his way quietly through the crowd. He moved effortlessly and unhurriedly in his blue button-down and beige chinos, a kind smile lightened his chiseled features as he headed toward the car.

The engine revved loudly then Jake reversed the sedan speedily back out onto the dark, quiet road. Pausing, Max shared a look of concern with Dylan, his hand stroking the greying hair at his temple before he changed course and casually made his way over to Kyra. Dylan nodded to Brian, with whom he'd been speaking, and headed in the same direction.

Dylan felt the curious glances of the staff, volunteers and visitors following him. The weekly dinner had finished nearly an hour ago. Most remained to have a few drinks, socialize and catch up on any new gossip. Whether intentionally or spontaneously, Jake provided them with plenty in regards to his relationship with Kyra.

As Dylan neared Max and Kyra, he caught the end of their hushed conversation through the garbled murmur of the crowd and the rhythmic beat of the cheerful music.

"I'm okay, Max. Jake must have changed his mind. He's just…being antisocial."

Max looked exhausted, his blue-grey eyes darkening. "I hope that's all it is. He needs a purpose. I'd thought working here might give him one, but…" Max shrugged tiredly and looked up at Dylan, his expression softening with relief. "Dylan here made a mean steak tonight as usual. Got plenty of compliments."

"And I missed out." Kyra grinned, but Dylan could see it took her effort.

Max shook his head, even though a jovial smirk curved his lips. "That you did, Kyra and you'll have to wait another whole week before getting the chance again."

Although concern still overrode his feelings, Dylan offered them both a friendly smile. "I reckon Kyra's the lucky one tonight. Eating at a fancy restaurant, easily tops my brilliant barbequing skills."

Kyra's grin weakened. "Yeah, but the atmosphere wasn't the same."

"Nor was the company." Dylan placed a hand on Max's shoulder supportively.

His chest ached at how quickly his boss became more serious.

"We've got a good family," Max agreed, glancing over at the jubilant guests. "I'm ever grateful to have found such an incredible group of people who share my passion."

Dylan wished Max could say the same for his son. It pained him to see his good friend injured by Jake's antics. Max glanced his way and then laughed sharply.

"Ignore me. I didn't mean to lead this conversation down Serious Street." He took a step toward the inquisitive crowd mingling closer to the buildings. "I guess I should keep doing the rounds, share my precious time. You know how popular I am." He gave a jokey grin and headed away.

Dylan watched as Max began a conversation with another small group of people, mostly volunteers, who were seated in lawn chairs furthest away from the music. As the group shared a laugh, Dylan relaxed and turned his attention back to Kyra.

Long dark lashes shielded her fascinating hazel eyes, eyes which seemed to grow more troubled as he caught their gaze. She tunneled her fingers through her lopsided bob, sweeping the strawberry blonde hair from her face as she pressed her luscious pink lips together in a tight line.

Dylan's chest tightened at the sight of her unhappiness. "Jake had better have been on his best behavior tonight."

Kyra nodded confidently. "He was."

"Didn't want to join the fun though?" Dylan gestured around at the people and then stuck his hands in the pockets of his midnight blue jeans.

As Kyra walked toward the accommodation building, Dylan strolled along beside her.

"Maybe he had somewhere better to be?" She was careful not to look at him.

Dylan wondered if her matter-of-fact tone was to convince him or herself.

"Where are you heading now?" He watched her closely as they stepped up onto the ground floor porch.

She gave him a shrug and his heart clenched. He could see she was hurting, but was trying to hide it. Still, she wouldn't look at him.

"Why don't we grab a couple of drinks, sit out the back and enjoy the night a while?"

She shrugged again, her shoulders moving up and down with her breath. "I'm tired," she began, her voice sounded a little hoarse as she rubbed a hand across her eyes.

Unable to contain himself, Dylan reached out, grabbed her hand and held it in his, forcing Kyra's beautiful hazel eyes – moistened and reddened now – to stare up at him.

"I know it's not just that," he told her, his hand still holding hers securely.

Her lips quivered and she took a deep breath, sighing it out loudly. "I'm fine." It was less than convincing.

He smiled down at her reassuringly. "You will be, once we've enjoyed the night air for a little while."

Kyra frowned at him, her gaze seemed to glint with inner turmoil, then she nodded decisively. "Out the back."

He nodded his head in agreement. "Out the back."

After arranging the lawn chairs so they faced the darkened wilderness behind the fenced line at the back of the property, Dylan and Kyra relaxed into them and clinked the necks of their beer bottles in cheers. Although the beat of the lively music was still evident behind them, they were far enough away from the jubilant crowd and their capers that they could hear the calming sounds of nature on the warm night air. The chirping of the crickets seemed to compete with the hum of the distant music and garbled chatter, while the soft croaking of a frog emanated from the enormous water tanks to their right.

Breathing deeply, Dylan inhaled the sharp, but pleasant smell of eucalyptus from the gum trees at the boundary and beyond, which wafted around them on a breeze slightly cooler than the humid night.

"I never get sick of this," he said on a sigh before glancing over at Kyra.

She took a sip of her beer and then gazed skyward. "Or them."

Looking up at the entrancing darkness of the moonlit sky, Dylan felt his chest swell in awe. Living out in the bushland and away from the bright lights of the city meant they had the privilege of seeing billions of stars not usually visible. It was as though someone had dusted the sky with gold and silver glitter. They sparkled down at the Earth, twinkling greetings to passing satellites that glowed radiantly as they traveled on by.

"I know what you mean. They ground me and remind me life and the universe is bigger than all of us. We should love, appreciate and respect what we have, what life has given us."

The words left Dylan's lips before he had a chance to think them through. He hadn't meant to get so deep and bare his soul because they were alone together, but being with Kyra seemed to bring it out of him. He shot a look at her, anxiety quickening his pulse.

"Sorry. Clearly, I'm an emotional drinker." He chuckled nervously and then forced the beer bottle to his lips before he could say anything even more humiliating.

"No. Don't be." Kyra shook her head at him. "I understand. I think that's why I'm so passionate about preserving our turtles. I know we are miniscule in the scheme of things. You know, in the lifespan of the world, the universe? But, I value what I have and I want to make a difference, if I can."

Dylan froze, beer to his lips and eyes wide. It wasn't so much that he hadn't expected her to understand what he'd meant – he knew she was exceptionally intelligent. Or that he hadn't known her passion for wildlife conservation ran so deep – as it was just one of the many things that enticed him to her. No, it was the fact her true feelings were so similar in concept to his own and insightfully accurate that it all seemed quite serendipitous.

He felt the heat of her gaze as she watched him. Lowering the beer, Dylan turned and met her heartfelt stare.

Kyra nibbled at her lower lip. "Guess we've got the emotional drinker thing in common. Sorry. I didn't mean to make things awkward."

He swallowed. "No," Dylan said the word and knew it was a lie. He hadn't realized he could love her any more than he already did, but her words had touched him deeply. "No," he said again. "It's okay."

She dropped her gaze from his and then returned her attention to the sky. "I'm grateful for you, Dylan. I need you to know." Her voice was quiet and cautious.

He offered her a small nod, but couldn't manage a word.

Appearing to take his answer as acceptance, she continued. "I know we have a connection, you understand me. I mean, *really* understand me." She paused, breathing deeply, her eyes closing for just a second. "What I want to say is…I'm lucky to have met you, to have you in my life. I really care about our friendship, about *you*." She glanced in his direction, but her eyes shied away from his. "I never want to lose that, Dylan. I can't."

He forced another nod. "Of course."

Although a warm contentment filled him as she'd begun, by the time she'd finished, a consuming dread hung heavy in his gut. Her words had hit him hard. She didn't want to jeopardize their special friendship, he understood that. It was obvious she needed his support now more than ever after her turbulent evening with Jake, but knowing that didn't lessen the pain. His heart ached, though he knew she was right. What they had now was better, safer. Yet, he couldn't help longing for more.

"I care about you, too," he told her as her gaze finally met his again. "And you need to know, you'll never lose me."

CHAPTER FOUR

Kyra watched the foamy, blue waves crash ashore on the long stretch of golden sand of Mon Repos beach before turning her back on the ocean and following Dylan inland. She kept her head down and her eyes fixed on his footprints in the sand dunes. She knew the lenses of her sunglasses, unlike his polarized aviators, weren't dark enough to keep her from being caught staring at his sexy behind, yet that was all she wanted to do – stare at him.

Dylan led her toward the inlet of seawater which fed into the Mon Repos Conservation Park, a sheltered piece of land that was a popular nesting area for the turtles. Even though the land was protected, terrestrial predators still posed a risk to the hatchlings, making the area a high priority for patrols. In the wake of the poaching, the patrols had increased further, with everyone on alert scouring the landscape for any signs of trespassers.

Although, Kyra hadn't been rostered to patrol again until tomorrow morning, when Dylan had asked if she'd be keen to accompany him after lunch today, she'd jumped at the opportunity to help. Or at least that's why she thought she'd agreed. Now, she wasn't so sure what her intentions were.

As they entered the patchy shade of trees, Kyra's gaze lifted and met the curve of Dylan's butt through the snug fabric of his khaki cargo pants before lifting, tracing an invisible line up his back, over his white singlet. When she got to his broad, muscular shoulders, she caught herself and dragged her gaze back down, silently scolding herself for the slip-up.

It wasn't as though she hadn't admired his appearance before, only a blind woman would be immune to his rugged attractiveness, but lately she could feel herself giving in to his magnetism. Ever since their time together a couple of nights ago, the night of her lackluster kiss with Jake, thoughts of Dylan had consumed her. She couldn't decide if her subconscious was punishing Jake for abandoning her or if something in her heart had changed. Then there was that kiss, gratifying, yet not quite right.

She shook her body, trying to shake the uneasiness from her limbs.

What was wrong with her? Jake was perfect. He was just the right percentage of bad-boy and a thimble full of playboy without being an outright ass. Coupled with a love of nature and a compassion for preservation and wildlife that mirrored her own, he was a perfect match for her, wasn't he?

Her thoughts irked her and she stopped walking.

Dylan strode a few more steps along the top of the dune, before he noticed she'd stopped. He frowned as he turned to face her.

"Did you see something?" He raised his sunglasses, resting them on top of his tousled, auburn hair before scanning the ground around them.

"No." She shook her head. "Sorry. Maybe I shouldn't have come. I'm feeling rather distracted."

"Why? What's wrong?" The worry in his features reached his eyes as he made his way back to her. He placed a warm hand on her bare shoulder and then glanced up at the hot afternoon sun. "Is it the heat? It's pretty humid again today. We might even get a storm."

Shaking her head, Kyra's brows knotted. "No. It's…" she sighed unable to verbalize the uneasy feeling. She grimaced in irritation. "It's just me."

He stepped closer, his free hand reached for her purple sunglasses and lifted them so he could see her eyes. He gazed down at her, his blue-green eyes full of distress as he studied her. "You're not feeling weak? Lightheaded?"

She pushed the glasses free of him to rest atop her head. "No." Her hand went to his chest, but she wasn't sure if she'd meant to push him away or just touch him. "I'm fine."

When he gave her a look of skepticism, she sighed and glanced down at her hand, feeling the firm muscle of his chest beneath her palm, his pulse beating beneath her fingertips. She snatched her hand back as though she'd been stung and forced her eyes back to his.

"I was thinking about the other night with Jake." She bit out the words and then mentally reprimanded herself for broaching the topic.

Why had she said that? Was she really seeking Dylan's opinion? Or had she wanted to see a flash of jealousy in his eyes?

He'd been so good around her, ensuring their relationship remained perfectly platonic. Yet, she knew he'd felt something spark between them. She'd noticed his lingering stares and was certain he took advantage of every opportunity to touch her, even though all contact remained fleeting and companionable. Kyra appreciated the fact he'd never obviously flirted or pushed himself on her. Dylan was a decent guy with strong ethics and he worked hard to commit to them. He'd never take advantage of her. So why did she suddenly want him to break his code, to give in to his feelings and prove them to her?

Kyra gritted her teeth as Dylan stepped back, his hand dropping from her shoulder to give her space.

"Ignore me." She tried to reassure him and stop him in his retreat. "I don't know what I'm talking about. I really shouldn't have come along."

His comforting smile was tight. "It's okay. I know how much Jake upset you on Sunday night. I don't mind if you want to talk about it."

Dylan's posture stiffened and she wondered if he'd really meant what he'd said.

"I think I'm just confused," she blurted out, not really knowing where she was going with the statement. Catching herself quickly, she started again. "*He* confused me. We were having a really good night, at least, I thought we were and then," she shrugged her shoulders, "he dropped me off at the Center with a lame excuse. He said he'd changed his mind and wanted to get another drink in town."

Jake's mobile phone had kept jingling throughout their date, first with the sound of incoming calls and then with the short, snappy chirrups of text messages. He'd made a point of ignoring them, but she'd noticed him glancing at the phone many times. She'd thought the calls might have been Max, but on arrival at the Merchant Marine Science Center, she'd begun to wonder whether it was another woman.

She'd never questioned him about it nor did she want to tell Dylan about it either. The calls were another thing that troubled her about Jake. With Dylan, she knew their trust was mutual, but with Jake, she'd never been quite sure.

"I'd noticed there had been some tension between the two of you lately," Dylan said as sympathy warmed his gaze. "But you need to know, Kyra, Jake has a tendency to be like that. Flaky. He struggles to commit to things. Max keeps hoping it's a phase, but I don't know. He's old enough to be making better decisions."

Kyra felt the sting of coming tears and lowered her gaze away from his.

"I keep feeling as though I should give him the benefit

of the doubt, but then I think about how easy it was for him to leave me." She heard the pain in her voice, but couldn't stop herself from continuing. The dam of emotions she'd kept contained over the past few days released. "I feel like leaving me, especially after a date, should've been a struggle, but it wasn't. I thought I mattered to him, but I'm not sure I do."

Dylan reached out, his hand going high on her shoulder, his thumb close enough to her neck to caress her lightly, calmingly. She leaned into his touch, enjoying the feel of his hand on her skin, savoring the comfort and serenity it offered her. Without thinking it through, she moved into his arms, her own wrapping around his waist as she hugged him close, relishing the human contact. He went rigid at her touch, the solid muscles of his torso locking before he relaxed into the embrace. His free arm slid around her back, while the hand at her shoulder slipped up behind her neck, gently pressing her head to rest against the warmth of his chest.

"You shouldn't give him an extra thought if he makes you feel like this, Kyra," Dylan all but purred soothingly into her ear. "I may not have Jake's extensive experience in the dating scene, but I have enough of an understanding to know if the person you care for is making you feel this way, then they aren't worthy of your affection."

He rested his head softly atop hers and cuddled her tighter.

As she nestled in his arms, Kyra breathed in his scent, enjoying the earthiness of his skin, the slight tartness of his sunscreen and the hint of the fresh smell of soap left behind from his morning shower. She knew what Dylan had said was true, Jake's actions and feelings were questionable, but she was still conflicted.

In Dylan's embrace, she struggled to think of Jake and remember why she was upset. She was disappointed, not only with Jake's behavior, but with the result of their kiss. What they'd shared was pleasant, but far below her hopes and expectations. Yet, just the sensation of being in Dylan's arms was causing desire to prickle against her skin and feverish lust curled in her belly, swirling lower. He was comforting her, caring for her and all she could think of was how her bare skin felt against the warmth of his and what his lips would be like pressed to hers.

"I know you're away from home here, Kyra," Dylan crooned to her, "but don't ever think you are alone. We're a family, we support each other."

His hand drew a trail up her back, from the waistband of her ivory shorts, over the fabric of her violet tank and along the softness of her skin. He caressed up and down her spine, sending tingles of electricity through her to pop rapturously at her peaked nipples.

"I know." Breathless, she closed her eyes as she reveled in the sensations. "I know you're here for me."

"Of course, I am," he assured her. "I worry about you with him, Kyra. Maybe one day he'll grow to be like his father, but until then he'll still be the same lazy, conceited asshole I've always known him to be."

Her body jerked at his words. She didn't want to admit it, but he was probably right.

"Sorry," he murmured. "I didn't mean to get so heated."

She pushed out of the comfort of his embrace, just enough to look up at his ruggedly handsome features and gaze into his empathetic blue-green eyes.

"I—" The word barely came out when she opened her mouth.

As she stared up into Dylan's eyes, at his angular cheekbones, that straight nose, the rough shadow of auburn stubble on his strong jaw, at those full, kissable lips, she found herself enthralled, captivated by the way her heart beat while in his arms. He was close enough she could take a leap and press her mouth to his, to sate the desire building inside of her. But should she? Were these feelings she had for him intensifying because of their natural chemistry? Or were they just a consequence of her lackluster kiss with Jake?

She closed her eyes against the painful, puzzling conflict between her heart and her head. Then she forced herself to step back and break the mesmerizing hold he had over her.

"I—," she began again, keeping her gaze low as she lifted a hand to slide her sunglasses back over her eyes, "I'm not sure that's really a fair assessment of Jake."

"Kyra." Dylan's tone was a mixture of defiance and regret. "Don't be naïve, you're too smart for that."

At his comment, a sharp pang pained in her chest and when he reached for her, she moved away, stepping around him to continue along the sand dunes.

"Kyra," he pleaded, but she didn't turn around.

"We're here to work, Dylan," she snapped, her hand raised over her shoulder to silence him. "Let's get on with—"

Her words trailed off as she saw *it*. The disrupted ground, the flagged marker half buried on its side, the unmistakable deep well in the golden sand, all the upsetting signs of another emptied nest.

*

"Number sixty-three?" A slender Asian woman with stylishly cropped black hair and vibrant yellow-framed glasses walked around the counter with a couple of heavy containers in a plastic bag. "Sixty-three?"

Kyra watched from beside the open doorway as a stoutly, bearded man inside the take-out shop stood up and collected his order of Chinese food.

As she turned back to face the quiet, Bargara street, her stomach rumbled loudly. It had been another arduous day, but at least, it was finally Friday night. After she'd discovered the third incident of poaching yesterday, the police had wanted to query every staff member from both

Centers in detail. *Had they seen anything? Heard anything? Noticed anything out of the ordinary? Anyone acting strangely?*

It had been exhausting answering questions, but was worth it. The loss of the turtle eggs hung heavy in her heart ever since the first nest had been ransacked. It infuriated her she couldn't do more. She'd felt so angry at her uselessness, she was completely drained and hopeless.

To make matters worse, she'd spent all her remaining energy avoiding Jake and Dylan. She wasn't yet ready to speak to either of them, mainly because she didn't know what to say. It wasn't Dylan's fault she couldn't make up her mind about her feelings and it wasn't Jake's fault she hadn't felt the connection she hoped for with him. After thinking it over, she'd even wondered if maybe he'd felt the same and had noticed the spark just wasn't there for them after the kiss.

She sighed deeply and slipped the paper take-out docket into the back pocket of her denim shorts, before rubbing her hands over her tired eyelids. All she wanted to do was eat some Chinese food and laugh at a romantic-comedy while she hid alone in her room.

"Sixty-four? Sixty-four?" The woman with the brightly colored glasses stepped outside the door beside Kyra and looked at her. "Sixty-four?" She asked Kyra directly, lifting up the plastic bag of food in her hand.

Kyra shook her head and wished she was the owner of that number. "No," she said, grabbing the ticket from her shorts and holding it up to show the lady her digits. "Sixty-six."

The woman nodded and moved on. "Sixty-four," she called out again.

"Looks like someone's getting a take-out fix."

Kyra recognized the familiar male voice immediately and wondered if she ignored him whether he'd keep on walking and leave her alone. She waited a few more seconds than was socially acceptable while trying to decide, but finally turned to face him.

"Hi, Jake."

His grin was wide and child-like as she greeted him. "Hi, yourself." Then his brown eyes roamed her face. "You look totally haggard. Tough day at the office?"

She shrugged and then yawned, covering her widening mouth with her hand. "Long day."

Jake tilted his head to the side, studying her. "Too bad. I was going to invite you for a drink at the bar." He removed his right hand from the front pocket of his black jeans to point further down the well-lit street. "My shout and all. But, I guess you're too tired, huh?"

Kyra nodded. "Yes, Jake. Too tired tonight." She hadn't meant for it to sound sarcastic, but it had.

"Shame," he said, stepping closer to her, his eyes darkening flirtatiously. "I have enough money for us to get a motel room." He waggled an index finger at her. "No drunk driving back to the compound."

Too weary to decide whether to laugh or be insulted, Kyra crossed her arms over her chest, flattening the feminine frills on her rose-pink blouse. Had he really expected her to jump at that?

She forced a small smile. "I'm glad you're doing the responsible thing."

He leaned back and raised his eyebrows. "Have to. If I get into trouble with the cops again, Dad will cut my allowance even more."

Kyra frowned drowsily and rubbed her fingertips over her left eyelid, then down her cheek. "Didn't he just raise it?"

Why was she even bothering to prolong the conversation? The sooner he left, the sooner she'd have her meal, head back to base for a movie and then bed.

Jake's eyes widened and then his brows knit tightly, causing deep grooves to form between them. "Yeah, he has. That's why I'm so flush, he raised my allowance. But, yeah…" He shrugged almost nervously and then grimaced. "Don't want to have less money though, you know?"

Kyra pushed hard for another smile. "You have a good night, Jake."

He flinched and then his face brightened cheerfully. "Yeah, you, too." He stepped around her and started to walk away. "Have a good night."

She nodded again and ignored the desire to shoo him quicker with her hand. "Bye."

He waved, then turned and sprinted away down the street.

"Sixty-six?"

The lady in the yellow glasses appeared beside her again, a plastic bag of food containers in hand. As Kyra swapped her ticket for the food and wished the woman goodnight, she suddenly realized she'd completely missed number sixty-five and was grateful for it.

CHAPTER FIVE

The hot morning sun beat down on Dylan's bare shoulders as the gentle waves of the blue surf helped to push his kayak further ashore. Before the strong orange plastic of the craft's hull hit and settled on the submerged golden sand, he swung his legs over the side and into the refreshingly cool, thigh-deep water. With an arm on the kayak, guiding it along, he waded toward Mon Repos beach. The long stretch of pristine sand appeared to be more crowded than a usual Sunday morning. The normally rough surf was more placid today with small, rolling waves curling to shore.

Laughing families created sand-sculptures, played beach cricket and splashed in the shallows, while teenagers and twenty-somethings tossed around a volleyball and sunbathed. Unpatrolled by lifeguards and a favorite nesting area for marine turtles, water play on the beach was often kept to a minimum and signage prevented human visitors from climbing up into the dunes. Dylan couldn't hide his smile as he admired the beachgoers and their unabashed enjoyment of the day. It always pleased him to see people appreciating and respecting their natural surroundings.

Having survived the stressful events of the past few

days, Dylan had spent his morning off travelling up and down the coast communing with nature. He'd needed to get away from everything and get his thoughts about the illegal poaching and his feelings for Kyra in order. Although there had been no breakthroughs to help catch the poachers, he knew everyone was doing their best to solve the problem. Even though he wished he could do more, he was confident the increased patrols, by both the rangers and police, would reveal something soon. It was only his dilemma with Kyra and his confusion over what to do next that troubled him.

Dylan loved having her in his arms and holding her close. Her soft curves had enticed him as he breathed in the floral fragrance of her hair and the sweet scent of her skin. Yet, he'd kept his desires to himself, even when she'd looked up at him, her lips parted as though waiting for his kiss. He'd been the *good guy* and then screwed everything up by insulting her. He hadn't meant for it to sound like an accusation, but his heart sagged in his chest when she'd backed away from him. Why had she continued to protect Jake? Surely, she must have seen his true colors.

He pushed away his annoyance, fighting with his train-of-thought, stopping it spiraling again. His lengthy paddle along the coastline had removed some of his frustration, but it hadn't helped him come to a decision about the woman he loved. He would have to wait for fate to intervene.

Once his kayak bucked against the sand, Dylan continued to drag it up and out of the water. It was common practice for him to carry it all the way up the beach, along the boardwalk and to the trolley he'd left padlocked to a fencepost in the parking lot, but today, he planned to make the most of the beautiful water, before starting the trek home. Leaving the sea craft secured in the softer sand beyond the tide's reach, Dylan turned and headed back out into the water. It was deliciously cold against the humidity of the day as it churned silkily around him.

When he was waist deep, his black shorts submerged, he heard a sound behind him. A muffled call – his name maybe? He spun around slowly, his whole body bobbing slightly as a salty wave raised the water level and then rolled past him to shore.

"The workaholic has finally decided to chill, I see." Jake's yell carried from where he strolled along the sand toward the kayak.

Dylan didn't think the smart remark deserved a response, nor did he want to leave the pleasure of the undulating ocean, but he inched closer to shore anyway.

"Nice kayak." Jake stopped beside the vessel, his hands resting low on his hips, over the waistband of his maroon shorts as he looked over it approvingly. When he glanced up again, his toothy grin was smug. "I'm thinking of getting the newer model. You know, the one with the padded seat and back rest. It's also got a detachable sunshade awning. Pretty cool, huh?"

Dylan twirled his fingers lightly through the velvet water around him as the force of another wave lifted him to his toes. "You've been saving then? I didn't think that was a skill in your repertoire."

"Yeah," Jake yelled in reply. "Something like that."

Dylan stared him down as the silence lengthened between them. He didn't want to have the jerk ruin his day of rest and couldn't understand why Jake was bothering to take the time to talk to him either. Neither was each other's favorite person. Even though Dylan did his best to get along with him to appease Max, Jake always pushed the limits.

Crossing his arms over his chest, Dylan's grimace tightened his jaw. "What do you want from me, Jake?"

Jake padded down to the water's edge, bare chest puffing slightly as though preparing his defenses. When his feet slipped into the shallows, he stopped, his grin twitching. "Don't think you could do me a favor, do you?"

Dylan should've predicted it. Of course, Jake wanted a favor. The entitled idiot always wanted something without offering anything in return.

"I wasn't aware we were the kind of people who did favors for each other." Dylan did his best to remain matter-of-fact.

"What kind of people? *Friends*?"

Jake's jovial expression didn't soften Dylan's even slightly.

"Fine." Jake clawed his fingers through his windblown, light-brown hair. "So, we're not. Doesn't mean you can't do me a favor?"

Dylan wanted to roll his eyes. "If you don't spit it out in the next few seconds, then the only answer you'll get will be no."

Jake threw up his hands, his expression morphing into desperation, then frustration. "Just tell Kyra I'm not a complete dick, will you?"

Dylan's left eyebrow shot up. "Excuse me?"

Jake stepped further into the water. "Kyra's good, you know? She's the best. I just don't want her to hate me."

"Maybe," Dylan began with a half-hearted shrug, "she won't think you're such a dick if you stop behaving like one."

Jake's unimpressed expression had Dylan's lips curving in a smile.

"Okay." Dylan heard the slight lilt of laughter in his voice and hoped Jake didn't notice. "I won't make you any promises. I'm not a liar, Jake. I won't lie for you, but maybe if you start helping out at the Turtle Center a little more with the extra patrols, maybe even put your name down to join those of us who are going to start camping out on the dunes until we catch those lowlifes, maybe then I'll start spreading the word about your good deeds."

Though the concept of talking up another guy to the woman he loved would never be high on Dylan's list of things to do, he had no problem offering credit where credit was due. If Jake bothered to get off his ass and help out, then Dylan would tell Kyra – even if it irked him to do so – of the change in his behavior.

Jake's hands went to his hips again. "You couldn't just say yes, could you?"

Dylan tilted his head. "Sure. To the right question."

He watched as Jake struggled, pondering over the offer. Dylan knew it wasn't too much to ask for Jake to act like a decent human being, but it was up to Jake to make the decision.

"Look, Jake, while you're contemplating the moral of your character, taking your sweet time, I'm wasting mine. Any chance you could speed it up?"

Jake frowned at him. "Fine. I'll check in with my dad, see what needs to be done around the Turtle Center. Happy?"

A small smile pulled at Dylan's lips. "It's not me you're trying to impress remember, it's Kyra."

Jake rolled his eyes.

"Baby steps are better than nothing, Jake," Dylan told him, sincerity deepened his tone. "You stick to your word and I'll stick to mine."

He didn't bother to wait for Jake's answer. By his understanding, their conversation was over. Dylan turned, letting the silky water trickle around him as another wave lifted him slightly and rolled on by. He took a couple of steps, then raised his arms as he bent and dived into the clear, blue abyss.

*

Although the wind had picked up, adding white-tips to the choppy waves, Kyra still thought it was a glorious Tuesday afternoon. The salty breeze blowing in over the Pacific Ocean invigorated her. The fluffy clouds didn't hinder the warmth of the sunshine on her bare skin.

She'd spent the whole day inside, testing samples in the

lab, and extrapolating population predictions on the computer, in addition to avoiding Jake and Dylan. Needing a break, Kyra drove down to Nielson Park Beach to get some much-needed vitamin D. After laying her pink towel on the sand and stripping down to her emerald bikini, she'd stretched out and dozed. She hadn't meant to, but the sun was so comforting. The sound of the waves curling to shore was so peaceful, she'd just drifted away.

Dazed upon waking, she was confused for a moment as to what time it was. The sun had yet to touch the horizon and she quickly realized her nap must've been shorter than she'd first thought.

With her sunglasses on, Kyra stood, slipped on her black short-shorts, then grabbed her towel and white singlet before heading back up the beach. As she climbed the sand dunes to the grassy embankment, she heard the throaty chuffs of male laughter.

"Kyra? Kyra!" A familiar croaky voice called.

She glanced up to see Brian and a group of four older, grey-haired men sitting on lawn chairs in the shade of the Bundaberg Surf Lifesaving Club's balcony. They were sun-loving men, real beachy-looking guys in their brightly colored button-downs, their faces tanned and deeply lined from their coastal adventures. Having run across the group at the shore before, she recognized them as Brian's old surf lifesaving buddies who often met up for a drink and a chat at their old stomping grounds.

Brian waved her over to them. "What are you doing here, Kyra?" He sounded genuinely curious.

"Just getting some sun."

He looked confused by her answer. "Jake somewhere nearby?"

Kyra frowned at the assumption. "I'm not his keeper."

Brian laughed as one of his mates, a man with shoulder long hair and a scraggly beard piped up. "Trouble in paradise, hey?" It earned him a commendation of laughter from the others.

"No," she drawled and fought the urge to poke her tongue out at him. "There's no trouble, there's no paradise. I'm here, he's elsewhere."

"Whatever you say," teased another of the gang, a slightly younger man with a reddish-tinge still in his hair, a man she vaguely remembered as Steve or Stu.

They laughed again, Brian less enthusiastically this time, and she didn't bother to validate the comment with a response.

When she raised a hand to wave them farewell, Brian stood abruptly, halting her retreat.

"Don't mind the boys, Kyra," he told her. "They're natural born stirrers and can't help themselves."

She shrugged and offered him a smile. "I know the type. My dad's got the same condition."

Brian grinned at her for a moment before his expression lost its shine.

"Look, I just wanted you to know that I only asked about Jake 'cause he said you and he were going out."

"Well, we're not," she explained. "We went out once."

Brian shook his head. "No. I was talking about tonight. See, I was outside the center about an hour ago. I'd gone to lend Dylan some camping gear. The zipper is busted on his sleeping bag and he's scheduled for camp out tomorrow." He waved a hand between them as though noticing he'd gone off track. "Anyway, Jake was talking to Max as I walked by. He got in his car, telling his father he couldn't patrol tonight 'cause he was going out to dinner and a movie with you."

Kyra considered what he'd said as Brian watched her reaction closely.

"That's where I thought you'd be, see?" His tone had changed, a seriousness, a suspiciousness deepening it. "I, at least, thought the two of you'd be together."

Kyra nibbled at her bottom lip. Why had Jake said that? Had he been meaning to ask her out, but never gotten around to it? Was he just trying to keep up appearances?

Or was he going out with someone else, another woman, the one who'd been calling him over and over?

"Yeah," Brian nodded as he assessed her expression. "Thought you'd find it interesting."

"I don't know what he was talking about," she said with a frown. "But, I can tell you that I'm keen to find out."

CHAPTER SIX

Kyra stuffed the last of her camping gear into a duffle bag as she heard the four-wheel drive's engine growl to life outside. Zipping the bag closed, she straightened her peach-colored singlet, pulling it down over her denim short-shorts as she quickly glanced around the room, checking she'd packed everything. Content, she slung the strap over her shoulder and grabbed the rolled-up sleeping bag off the bed. Once she'd exited her room, she locked the door and then hurried downstairs to the driveway. As she headed over to the tall, silver-colored vehicle with the Merchant Marine Science Center's name and logo on the side, she could hear the thumping beat of music emanating through the closed, tinted windows. It had been another hot day and Kyra thought Sandra, who'd been rostered with her to camp out in the dunes tonight, was probably enjoy the iciness of the car's air-conditioning.

Even though Sandra was almost twenty years her senior and had two young children, they'd bonded quickly over reality television and Italian food, their admitted guilty pleasures. Since Sandra was a ranger based at the Turtle Center, Kyra didn't get to see her as often as the team at the Science Center and had been looking forward to a girls' night out camping with her. Maybe she'd even be able to get a few things off her chest about her guy troubles.

Opening the trunk, Kyra threw her stuff beside the other bags and a packed tent, before closing it and coming around to open the passenger-side door. As Kyra placed her foot on the side step, ready to climb into the vehicle, she glanced up at the driver.

Dylan's handsome face grinned at her as he turned down the radio's volume. "Ready to go on your first stake-out?"

She paused for a split-second. Her heart raced at the surprise, before lowering her bottom to the cushioned seat. "I thought I was rostered with Sandra?"

He frowned. "Max hasn't told you?"

She sighed, unable to hide her disappointment. "Sandra can't make it?"

He nodded as he jerked the gearstick out of park and drove slowly up the long driveway toward Mon Repos Road. "Belle's too sick to be left with a babysitter and Sandra's ex is back at the mine in Dawson this week." After pulling out onto the bitumen of the minor road, Dylan glanced quickly in her direction. "I'd thought about saying no, but there was no one else to do the shift at the last minute."

A tug of remorse pulled at her belly. Even though she'd been avoiding him to have some time to get her own thoughts and feelings in order, she hadn't meant for him to feel forced to do the same. It wasn't as though she didn't want his company. She couldn't tell if the feelings she had were true and she didn't trust herself around him.

"I'm glad you didn't," she looked over at him quickly, "say no, I mean."

She prayed he understood she wasn't upset with him. Sure, his comment had made her so mad, but why? Looking back especially after having some space, she agreed with his analysis both of Jake and herself.

Maybe she was naïve when it came to Jake. He was definitely lazy, pretty obviously conceited, so why couldn't he be an asshole as well? After finding out from Brian that Jake had lied to his father about his whereabouts and dragged her reputation into it, Kyra had been more than livid with him. But she hadn't been able to find him to tell him and give him a chance to fumble around for some explanation. Two days later and he had yet to show himself. Maybe Brian had confronted him and now he was laying low until he thought she'd be in a better mood to hear him out. Or maybe he was still out spending time with that woman who wouldn't stop calling him.

"Me, too," Dylan agreed quietly, taking his gaze from the road for just a moment to offer her a smile. "I can't think of a better partner for a stake-out."

Proving he really was the 'mountain man' Kyra had always thought he appeared to be, Dylan set up their eco-friendly campsite in record time. Their green and grey colored tent was small, but big enough to house two sleeping bags side-by-side with room at the entrance for their belongings. Since the area they occupied was part of the protected land near the inlet in the Mon Repos Conservation Park, they couldn't light a ground fire. Instead they'd lugged a battery lantern and small portable stove along with the other camping gear up from the parking lot. They were also equipped with a flare gun in case of an emergency. While staff and volunteers were there as a deterrent only, the gun provided a simple means of notifying the patrolling police cars and the other teams camped out on the beach, or an option to scare off the egg-pinching douchebags.

Dylan and Kyra decided to settle themselves in a central location between three large clutches. All three had been flagged as significant due to the above average number of turtle eggs. While there was no guarantee the poachers would show up at the spot or on a clear, starlit night, Dylan had suggested it was likely one of these nests was the next target and Kyra agreed.

"You can cook on that thing?" Kyra made a weak attempt to hide her smirk.

Dylan appeared strangely domestic as he sat on a folding chair and tended to the frypan on top of the portable stovetop. He used an egg turner to flip a fried egg and grinned over his shoulder at her.

"You know I have incredible cooking skills," he teased.

She couldn't dispute that. He'd wowed her several times when he'd made dinner for the team at the compound, but he hadn't looked so...well, so damn sexy.

Tonight, he was wearing those khaki pants, the ones with all those pockets which made him look more military than park ranger. His tight, black T-shirt was snug around his muscular form. She'd seen him in the same clothes many times before but she'd never appreciated the sight more.

She moved closer and sat beside him in a second folding chair. The sun had set shortly after they'd set up camp and had given way to the beautiful midnight blue of the night sky. Though the moon had yet to rise, the stars above them twinkled, adding light to the glow of the portable lantern. Kyra watched as Dylan scooped her eggs onto a plate with fried toast and turned to face her.

"Eggs à la camp stove." He presented the plate to her.

She laughed and took it from him. "Thanks, Chef."

He winked at her before flipping a couple of eggs on his own plate and turning off the stovetop. As he leaned back in his chair, he poised his knife and fork above his meal.

"I really am sorry about the other day, Kyra. You know that, right?"

Surprised by his sudden acknowledgement of the incident, Kyra froze mid-mouthful. When he looked up at her as though seeking an answer, she chewed quickly, covering her lips with her hand as she nodded and then swallowed loudly.

"I know." The words came out choked and she coughed to clear her throat. "I know, Dylan. It's okay."

He shook his head, then lowered it to look at his food. "I shouldn't have said any of it. Your relationship with Jake is none of my business. I was just worried about you."

Kyra shrugged. "There's no relationship, Dylan. In fact, Jake will be lucky if there's still a friendship when he next shows his face." Her gaze dropped to the meal in her lap and she took another bite of toast.

Through her peripheral vision, she noticed him playing with his food, pushing an egg around his plate.

"Can I ask why?" It sounded as if he'd chosen his words carefully.

"I think he's seeing someone else." Kyra sighed and gazed over at the tranquil water of the dark inlet a few yards downhill from them.

Being far inland meant they were sheltered from the choppy wind stirring up the ocean along the coast, but the crash of the waves on the beach at the edge of the Conservation Park was still audible. As a cool breeze rustled through the mangrove forest higher on the sand dune beside them, the crickets chirped cheerfully.

Kyra shivered.

"Not that it matters," she sighed, focusing back on her dinner. "I'm beginning to think the Jake I thought he was, might not actually exist."

"What made you think that?" His tone remained wary, but now held a lilt of sympathy.

She glanced up at him, her eyebrow quirking from curiosity. "You're not going to say you told me so?"

He frowned. "No. I genuinely want to know what the idiot did to mess things up with a such an incredible, irresistible woman like you."

Something warm clutched at Kyra's heart and she was helpless to stop the heat of blush from pinkening her cheeks. *An incredible, irresistible woman.* Was that how he saw her?

"Crap. Sorry," he slapped a hand over his face. "Now, I'm the idiot."

"No," Kyra said quickly. She reached a hand out to him, but then stopped, pulling it back uncertainly. "No. It's okay," she began again. "Um…he's just been acting a little strangely. He lied about his whereabouts the other evening. Said I was with him, but I wasn't. I'm pretty sure he's seeing someone else, someone who keeps calling him, but maybe he doesn't want Max to find out? That's all."

Dylan gave her a weak smile. Something in his handsome blue-green eyes seemed to suggest he was grateful she'd ignored his remark.

"Jake has a bit of a reputation as a lady's man," he said as though he were trying to be delicate of her feelings.

"You don't say," she said almost teasingly.

His smile widened. "Sorry. Maybe we should change the subject." He picked up a piece of toast and then pointed it at her. "So, what do you think about the Bundaberg region?"

Kyra watched him unwaveringly, her gaze holding his as she sucked up the courage to ask what she'd been wanting to ever since their night under the stars. "Bundaberg's lovely, Dylan," she told him. "What do you think about me?

His eyes became large and he looked anxious, like a trapped animal.

"I know you like me," Kyra continued, while butterflies frolicked in her gut. "You just called me an incredible woman. So then, why haven't you said anything? Why not ask me out?"

He opened his mouth, coughed nervously and then stood, leaving his plate on his chair as he turned his back on her. She watched as he ran a hand through his hair before turning to face her again.

"Because I'm a decade older. Because I'm supposed to

be your mentor. Because it's *wrong*."

She rose to her feet, abandoning her meal on the folding chair behind her and went over to him. "A decade isn't an eternity, Dylan. Twenty-two and thirty-two are closer than you think and sure, you are my mentor, but it isn't wrong. I was never informed of any policies around staff and intern relationships. There's three married couples working at the Centers and two of them met on site."

Kyra reached a hand out to his arm, but he flinched away.

"I don't want to do anything to break your trust, Kyra." His deep, velvety voice sounded pained. "I have to protect you. You said yourself our friendship was important to you, that you didn't want to lose it."

Her heart swelled at his words. He *was* one of the good ones, she'd known it all along. Yet, now that she'd confirmed it, she wasn't about to let him pull away again.

"This won't mean that I'll lose you, Dylan," she said softly, trying to convince him. "This could be better."

"I don't want to be your rebound," he said sharply, but his eyes quivered with concern.

She reached out for him again and this time, her hand fell against the bare skin of his forearm. Her fingers caressed him reassuringly.

"You're not my rebound." The butterflies in her stomach filled her chest with elation and desire. "Dylan, I think you might be the one I was looking for all along, someone to share my passion with, my perfect match."

She watched as a myriad of emotions played out over his gorgeous features – anger, happiness, determination, and fear. His blue-green eyes filled with tenderness and then resolve.

"Screw it." He growled as he grabbed her, pulled her against him and captured her mouth with his.

He tasted salty, savory like the butter from his toast as his tongue danced with hers. His passion mesmerized her and sent rolling waves of lust to shatter through her, curling her toes. Electricity tingled through her whole body at his touch, causing her head to spin. She clung to him. Her heart raced with joy. Everything felt *right*.

CHAPTER SEVEN

Dylan wasn't sure if it was the flash of torchlight that woke him or the swishing sound, like footsteps in the sand. Either way, he was grateful, because the crickets weren't chirping.

After breaking his moral code and kissing Kyra, the atmosphere of the entire night had rapidly changed. They'd finished dinner, cleaned and packed everything away in record time, before she had taken his hand and pulled him into the tent. Although he'd done his best to remain in control and not let things go too far, he'd struggled – boy, had he struggled. Her kisses were addictive and touching her was utter ecstasy. Even though a small part of him still argued it was wrong, the rest of him knew it *was* right.

As he cuddled Kyra in his arms, she rubbed her cheek affectionately against his bare chest, making him smile contentedly. Hearing the sound again, he pressed his lips to her ear.

"There's someone outside," he breathed.

Her beautiful eyes fluttered open and she looked up at him in the dark. "Poachers?" Dylan wasn't sure if he'd heard the word or if she'd just mouthed it.

He nodded. Who else would be wandering the protected land in the middle of the night?

He sat up slowly, while she did the same. He grabbed his black shirt and her singlet from where they'd been thrown to the side. Passing hers, Dylan slipped his over his head and climbed quietly out of the sleeping bag. He was grateful for his self-restraint, which had kept them sensibly dressed below the waist. Then he took the flare gun from where he'd kept it safe in its heavy-duty Pelican case. He slid his feet into his brown boots, then watched her strap on her sandals before he slowly unzipped the tent flap.

As he climbed outside into the moonlit night, Dylan had an urge to tell Kyra to stay put. There was no need for her to abandon the safety of the tent to investigate the noise. But, he knew Kyra too well. He'd tried many times previously to protect her when there'd been shark sightings before their dives, yet she'd never listened. No, he'd be better off keeping his macho thoughts to himself, then maybe she'd at least stay behind him.

Dylan focused on the noise, a swishing like shifting sand and then a rustling, a crinkling sound like that of a plastic bag. He only had one flare as he hadn't thought to grab a second from the case. If he did this right, he'd be able to shoot the flare above the nest and scare off whoever was nearby.

He felt Kyra's hand touch his side reassuringly. As he glanced back at her, he moved his hand to his ear, gesturing for her to listen before returning his attention to the shadowy sand dunes in front of them.

Suddenly, there was a throaty murmur, followed by another. Kyra's hand pressed harder into his side until he glanced back at her. With her standing nearby, he could see her eyes widen as she pointed south-west to the flagged nest furthest from them. Dylan nodded his agreement before motioning for her to follow him. They climbed the dune until they were in line with the darkness and security of the nearby mangrove forest and then inched silently closer in the direction of the voices. He wanted to get close enough to ensure the flare struck overhead, lighting up the nest and the poachers before they ran off. If he and Kyra were lucky, they might be able to get a good description to pass onto the police.

As they neared the spot, Dylan saw the dark outlines of two people crouched low on the dune. The deep voices were louder now but still indistinguishable. Certain they'd reached a good position where they'd be safe, he stopped and held up a hand to halt Kyra. Making sure she was still behind him under the cover of the trees, Dylan stepped out enough to allow his aim to clear the branches and leaves above. With the gun securely in his hand, Dylan raised his arm over the direction of the nest. His finger itched on the trigger.

Electronic music pierced the silence like the chirruping noise of a cellphone. Dylan froze and glanced over at the gloomy figures as a disgruntled bird squawked its disapproval and flew out of the mangroves nearest the poachers.

"Crap! Will you turn that racket off?" The voice was louder this time, deep, husky, and clearly male.

One of the figures stood, appearing to fumble for a moment. The volume of the catchy tune increased. Convinced the poachers still hadn't seen them, Dylan returned focus back on his mission. He looked up, quickly corrected his aim and then fired. The melodious music ceased a split-second before the echoing blast of the flare rang out into the night.

"What was that?" It was a different voice this time, still deep, still male, but sharper, younger and he sounded worried.

Dylan stepped back under the cover of the mangroves as soon as he'd shot the flare skyward. He watched and waited silently, his hand holding tightly onto Kyra's to keep her with him.

There was a loud fizzing bang like the crackling of a

firework as the flare reached its peak and exploded into a vibrant red and orange flame.

"Shit!" The younger man shouted. "Oh no, shit! Oh, God."

While the effervescent flare began to fall, its incandescent color illuminated the ground below, lighting up the poachers and the pillaged nest almost as clear as day.

An older, robust man with dark hair, black slacks and a grey windbreaker jumped to his feet as he glanced at the sand dunes and the quiet inlet around them. "We've got to go," he growled as he clutched a black garbage bag in his fist.

"No! I've dropped it." The younger man yelled. "It's in the nest. It's in the nest!"

From where he and Kyra were huddled close to the trunks of the protective mangrove trees, Dylan watched the younger man closely. He was slender, athletic, with light colored hair, a navy T-shirt and dark jeans.

"We've got to go!" The older man grabbed his accomplice by his shirt and pulled him backward. "We've got to get out of here!"

The older man stumbled in the soft sand as he shoved the other man southward, toward the cover of more mangroves and in the vague direction of the Mon Repos walking track. While the poachers struggled to make their escape, Dylan glanced skyward. The flare should land in the soft sand, out of harm's way. As Dylan watched the dark shapes of the poachers meet the refuge of the distant trees in the red glow of the flare's light, a siren began to wail.

"The police," Kyra whispered, her hand gripping his tightly.

Dylan glanced back at their tent. It was only thirty yards or so away, just over the rise. He had to get back there, get to the radio and call into base so they could pass their information onto the police. He was pretty sure the men were heading back to the walking track and almost certain they'd parked somewhere around Nielson Park Beach as the trail continued out of the forest there.

He turned, kissed Kyra lightly on the lips and then looked deep into her eyes. "Stay here," he ordered, he didn't want to risk her being seen if the poachers doubled back.

But, even as he said it, he knew he'd made a mistake.

*

Kyra just had to look. She needed to see what was left behind. Dylan wanted her to stay put in case the poachers returned, but she just couldn't help herself. She knew she should leave any evidence for the police. But, what if the poachers came back to take what they'd left behind? Then what would the police have? Surely, her finding what the poacher lost could be helpful, even if it meant her fingerprints were on it – whatever *it* was.

Hunching low, Kyra ran out from the trees. The flare still burned brightly from where it had landed in the sand a few strides right of the nest, setting the night aflame with gaudy reds, pinks and oranges. She could hear the police sirens wailing and growing louder as they neared. When she reached the nest, she slid down onto the sand, feeling grains of it work further into her sandals and up into her shorts. She looked down into the darkened hole and found she could see well enough from the remaining light of the flare to make out its contents.

Although the clutch of eggs had been disturbed by the poachers, it appeared the majority of them remained. They'd been lucky in their timing. Kyra noticed a long dark shape poking out of the sand beside the eggs. As she pulled it free, she realized what it was – a mobile phone.

The younger man must've dropped it when the flare had exploded. Kyra looked at the shiny black screen and pressed the button on the bottom of the device. As though saving power, it lit up only slightly to reveal a locked display with three message squares, all from a person by the name of *Jay*.

Kyra couldn't help but grin. The police could trace the number and hopefully find the douchebags who were responsible for organizing and committing the illegal poaching.

As she climbed to her feet, she saw Dylan running over to her, a worried look clouding his expression. She heard him talking into the transceiver radio as he neared.

"Thanks, Brian. We'll stay here until the police arrive. Over and out."

Then she noticed the sirens had changed. They sounded as though they were heading away.

Dylan clipped the radio onto his belt as he reached her. "Are you okay?" Concern choked his voice.

Kyra hadn't expected it. She'd been certain she'd be in for a scolding as usual, but he didn't appear mad, only fear-stricken.

When she nodded, he grabbed her and pulled her close, his arms wrapping around her, holding her tight.

"I was so worried," he told her. "I know what you're like." It came out sounding like a nervous chuckle. "I should've told you the opposite of what I wanted you to do."

"I'm fine," she said, but when he wouldn't let her go, she told him again. "Really, Dylan, I'm fine."

He released her slightly to look her over and then brushed her strawberry blonde hair from her eyes.

"Okay," he said with a small smile. "Then we should get back to the trees. Who knows whether or not the poachers will risk coming back."

He grabbed her free hand, then turned and started to pull her with him.

"Wait." She yanked his hand, making him stop and look back at her.

Kyra held up the phone in her hand.

Dylan glanced at it and then back at her. "What? Your phone?"

She grinned and shook her head. "No. Not my phone."

His eyebrows furrowed for a second and then realization seemed to dawn. "Not your phone," he repeated.

Dylan reached for it and then flinched his fingers away. He frowned at her. "Fingerprints."

She shrugged. "I had to get it. What if they'd come back?"

The phone vibrated in her hand and a familiar electronic chirruping began. The screen brightened dramatically and the name *Jay* appeared above the option to answer or decline the call.

She shared a look with Dylan, knowing her eyes were bound to be as wide as his. Should she answer it? What would she say?

With a scowl, Dylan nodded at her again. "Answer it."

Kyra bit down on her lower lip as she used her thumb to swipe the green answer button and then raised the phone to her ear. Dylan leaned in close beside her.

"Hello? Where the hell are you guys? You better not be down there. If you are, I'm pulling out. I'm not about to get caught because of your stupidity."

Kyra's body jerked at the familiar voice as Dylan turned to look at her, his blue-green eyes wide and his mouth contorting in surprise, then fury.

How could he do this? How could he betray everything that was supposed to be important to him?

Kyra was just about to scream into the phone and verbally eviscerate the complete asshole on the other end who was betraying his own proclaimed passion, when Dylan shook his head and put his finger to his lips.

Dylan was right, of course. They didn't want him to know they knew and couldn't have him high tailing it interstate or further. He was just as guilty as those guys who were doing all of the dirty work and needed to be caught and tried as such.

Placing his fingers around her hand, Dylan used his thumb to help hers slide over the button to end the call. When the phone beeped to signal the call had ceased and silence ensued, Dylan sighed deeply as disappointment furrowed his brow.

"Looks like he didn't need his friends' stupidity to get caught," he told her, wearily, "Jake had enough of his own."

CHAPTER EIGHT

Friday morning brought with it many tears of heartache and betrayal, but none of them were shed by Kyra. She was enraged by the destruction of Jake's actions and his lack of regard for the natural world. Although he'd pleaded with everyone and begged for their forgiveness when the police had escorted him away, she'd known he'd do it again exactly the same. Money spoke to him, nature didn't. Kyra was so angry she hadn't realized it before. She hadn't recognized the signs. He'd had more money lately, but still it hadn't clicked in her head.

Kyra sighed for the thousandth time as she cuddled closer to Dylan, resting her head against the calming warmth of his chest. They were lounging on the sofa in the communal kitchen at the Science Center compound. Although they'd already answered questions for the police throughout the night, the investigating officers had left but requested they get some rest before returning to the station in the afternoon.

As Dylan brushed the hair from Kyra's eyes and kissed the top of her head, Max walked into the room. His thick greying-brown hair was tousled in disarray. His blue-grey eyes were sunken and reddened. When he noticed the couple, he offered them a small smile.

"At least some good has come out of this mess," Max said, his tired tone brightening a little. "I wondered how long it'd take for you two to end up together."

Dylan lifted his head from Kyra's. "You're okay with this, then?"

Max frowned and looked instantly more tired. "Why wouldn't I be? You two have me believing in soul mates." He chuckled half-heartedly.

Kyra looked up to see Dylan's smile of relief.

"I'm glad," he told Max. "Now that I have her, I don't think I could give her up."

Max laughed. "No need, my friend. Just invite me to your wedding."

Kyra smiled and laid a kiss on Dylan's throat as a warm, contented feeling swelled in her chest. Could it really be a future possibility? *Their* wedding?

Dylan wrapped his arm tighter around her. "I'm really sorry about Jake, Max."

Kyra heard the pain and sorrow in his voice. She knew Dylan wished things had ended differently, as they all had. But, Jake had made his choices, and hopefully, he would learn from them.

Max leaned against the kitchen counter and rubbed his fingers over his eyelids. "Me, too," he said, despondently. "Me, too." When he glanced up again, he appeared to force his expression to become more cheerful. "I used to tease him about sending him to military school for more discipline." His lips quirked upward at the memory and then faltered. "Well, he'll certainly get it, if he gets jail time."

"Do you know how much time he's likely to get?" Dylan asked the question cautiously, obviously trying not to upset Max any further.

"The maximum sentence appears to be two years or a quarter of a million fine – possibly both." He sighed deeply. "His lawyer believes he can get the sentence reduced since Jake was never involved in the physical act of poaching, he'd only offered up information. However, there's no guarantee he'll escape jail time altogether."

Dylan pulled away from Kyra and stood.

"It'll be okay, buddy," he told Max reassuringly as he walked over to him.

Frowning sadly, Max shrugged.

Dylan opened his muscular arms wide and pulled the older man into an affectionate embrace. When Max reciprocated, Dylan patted him softly on the back.

"Jake's a big boy," Dylan said. "He can handle whatever's thrown at him. He can learn from this. We will help him. We'll get through things together, Max. That's what families are for."

Max wiped at his eyes, before pulling out of Dylan's compassionate hug.

Max smiled warmly at Dylan. "I knew I hired you for some reason," he teased as he slapped Dylan's shoulder gently. Then he glanced over at Kyra. "Well, I should get some rest, we all should, before we're needed at the copshop again."

He patted Dylan's shoulder once more as he gave him a look of tender appreciation and then headed for the door. When he reached the threshold, he glanced back and offered them both a pained smile, before tapping the doorframe with his hand and exiting the room.

Kyra's heart ached for him. Max had done his best with Jake. But they were very different people with very different priorities.

"We should probably do what he said," Dylan drawled tiredly as he moved back to the sofa and took hold of her hand. He tugged her from the softness of the cushions and up into his arms.

Kyra loved his hard body against hers, holding her and protecting her in his arms. It felt so perfect, so right. It was where she belonged.

Her heart fluttered in her chest as she gazed up into his

handsome blue-green eyes. "And what then?"

He kissed her lightly on the lips. "Then we go answer some more questions."

She slid her hands along his black T-shirt and over the muscles of his back, enjoying the feel of his body beneath her fingertips. "And after that?"

A smile teased at the corners of his mouth as he kissed her lips again, lingering a little longer. "Then," he said slowly, as though drawing out his answer, "I think it's time we go out on a real date."

Kyra struggled to keep the enthusiastic grin from her face. A proper date. This time with someone who shared her passions, who supported her dreams, and who truly cared about her. *The right man. Her perfect match.* She kissed him, her mouth dancing with his as her insides melted with joy and she all but swooned into his embrace.

The End

SNEAK PEEK AT PERSUADING LUCY

Chapter One

Juggling three glasses and a bottle of white wine, Lucy Spencer wove her way through the crowd engulfing the Riverside Tavern on Friday evening. As she tried to push quickly through the throng of obstinate people, she immediately regretted having chosen to wear her bandage dress to the occasion. She hadn't been out for drinks with her work friends in a long while and had been trying to make an effort with the green figure-hugging number.

When she finally reached their table, Lucy breathed a sigh of relief, free from the lively horde. Then, at the sight before her—heads bowed low over an electronic device—she frowned and quickly noted her mistake. Leaving her mobile phone alone on the table now seemed an obviously poor decision. She had thought it would be safe for a few minutes, but that had proved time enough for her good friends to snoop.

Lucy gently placed the glasses on the tabletop and began to pour the wine, trying desperately to ignore the uneasy feeling filling her stomach. Rosie's bleached blonde curls and plump cleavage bounced as she glanced up quickly to greet her. With a grin teasing at her rouged lips, Rosie nudged the taller, lankier young woman beside her with an elbow. Steph's colorful pixie cut was still bowed over Lucy's phone for a moment longer and then she glanced up to aim a sharp smirk across the table.

With a careful push from her index finger, Steph slid the device closer to Lucy. "Luce," she said innocently. "What's a *bome*?"

A flock of overly energetic butterflies buzzed around in

Lucy's gut. She had hoped to keep at least this secret separate from her working life. Nerves got the better of her and it became difficult to swallow. Making an effort to appear nonchalant, Lucy brushed the straight chocolate strands of her shoulder-length bob free from her neck.

Steph quirked an eyebrow at the action and her expression became playful. "And why does he miss *playing ninja* on the beach volleyball courts?"

Rosie spat out a laugh and snorted, which only encouraged Steph to release the quiet chuckle she'd been trying to contain.

"Okay. Okay." Lucy perched her slender figure on an empty barstool and then raised her hands to silence them. "Ha-ha. It's all very funny, but it's not what you think."

She spun her mobile phone around and glanced at the screen. Several messages in a conversation with her best friend Maddy appeared.

Maddy: *Your loving bome has called again, begging for your phone number. Apparently, he had a dream about the old days. You two playing ninja on the beach volleyball courts or something. He said he misses it. He misses you. Anyway, call me.*

Lucy: *Tell him he can take his fond memory and shove it up his womanizing ass!*

Maddy: *Are you ever going to talk to him again? You know he still doesn't know why you stopped.*

Maddy: *Luce? Maybe I should just give him your new number and be done with it.*

Lucy swore and her two friends were lost to hysterics once more.

As she madly messaged Maddy back, Lucy noticed Steph move forward, the fabric of her black Ponte jacket creasing as she leaned her elbows on the table. Even though she tried not to be obvious, Lucy was sure Steph had seen the reply *"don't you dare"* before it had been sent out into the universe.

"So, are you gonna confess or what, Luce? Who is this guy she's talking about? And what is a *bome*?"

Lucy sighed in frustration and placed her mobile phone back on the table. She frowned up at Steph and then rolled her turquoise-blue eyes. "Bane of my existence," she said.

Steph's curious expression brightened, and she relaxed her long, wiry frame back into her seat.

"Clever," cheered Rosie.

"So, out with it? Who is he and what's the deal?" Steph rubbed her hands together eagerly.

A heavy dread seemed to weigh against Lucy's insides as she realized she didn't have much choice in the matter at hand. She could tell the girls now or put up with their constant inquiries every day at work until she caved. Knowing them well meant Lucy knew they wouldn't give up until they had enough gossip to satisfy them. Releasing an almost never-ending sigh, Lucy resigned herself to the task.

"He—the bane of my existence—is an old former friend of mine. We became friends in middle school. We were best friends until senior year and then I cut off all contact with him when I went to college."

Shifting her short buxom figure to the edge of her chair, Rosie leaned her elbows on the table and frowned forlornly. "What happened?"

"It must have been something pretty crappy for you to shun him in such a way," Steph said before taking a sip from her glass of wine.

Lucy looked down at where her hands rested on the table. Unconsciously, she had begun to pick at her fingernails—not ripping, but fiddling. Just thinking about the reason aroused feelings of anger and betrayal. The emotions washed over her, burning through her as if the situation had happened only yesterday, not nearly a decade and a half ago. She took a deep breath and blurted out the transgression.

"I'd thought we were friends. Great friends. Then he

started to make his way through my girlfriends, dating one by one as if it were a sexy schoolgirl smorgasbord. He would never date any one in particular for a long period of time, but almost always left a broken heart in his wake and a crying mess that I had to clean up."

"What a bastard," spat Rosie.

Steph narrowed her gaze. "And never once did that include you?"

Lucy frowned. "We were just friends."

You can't hide from destiny....

Callum Hawthorne is one of those lucky guys who seem to have it all. He's a wealthy property tycoon, the CEO of his family's company. He's handsome, intelligent and charming and has a gorgeous new woman on his arm every week. But there's one thing still missing – the love of his life, Lucy Spencer.

Fourteen long years ago, Lucy left for college and cut off all contact with Cal, leaving their mutual friend Madison as his only connection. That was until in his effort to save his deceased father's beloved Gold Coast property, The Calypso, Cal contacts Insight Marketing, the best advertising firm in Melbourne, and discovers his Lucy among the team.

Successful marketing executive, Lucy Spencer had managed to avoid her ex-best friend for nearly half their lives. Fearful of trusting him, loving him and having her heart broken all over again, Lucy tries to keep her distance from him, but discovers that there is a fine line between love and hate, and maybe – just maybe – Cal could be her inescapable destiny.

Available at all major retailers

SNEAK PEEK AT DRAWN TO HIM

Chapter One

The tiny bell on the front door of the store tinkled portentously in the quiet calm of the room as it announced the arrival of a new customer. Finishing the careful stroke on the canvas in front of her, Erica Townsend turned to her small, mostly-elderly class.

"Using the same brush, continue your vertical strokes, adding more tree trunks to our scene." She motioned to the enlarged photograph of a sylvan landscape, which was clipped atop her own wooden easel.

As several of her students nodded, Erica pointed to a rotund gentleman with a tartan beret in the back row. "No need to go overboard, Hamish. Less is more at times, remember?"

He touched the tip of his hat in salute, while the others continued in their work.

Beside him, a ginger-haired woman wearing a blotchy smock pointed her paintbrush in Erica's direction. "I'll keep an eye on him for you, sweetheart."

"Thanks, Jocelyn."

Winking at the older woman, Erica climbed to her feet and rounded the wall of open shelves separating her store, Unique Art Boutique, into two individual spaces. Leaving the classroom behind, she entered the gallery and purchasable art supplies part of the shop. It still gave her a warm feeling, seeing her dream fulfilled. She had wanted to establish a place where her passion for art—creating it, teaching it, displaying it—could be enjoyed and shared by all. Then five years ago, needing to escape Brisbane after her mother's passing and another failed relationship, she'd come to the idyllic little town of Montville in the Sunshine Coast Hinterland in Queensland, and done just that.

Erica smoothed her hands over her white apron, now mottled with different hues of dried paint, hoping to remove the residue of green goop on her fingers before it ended up on her denim shorts or gray tank top. She didn't have many clothes left which weren't in some way stained by her profession.

Approaching her customer from behind, taking in the baby pink dress draped over the feminine figure, Erica smiled. "Can I help you?"

"Yes." The young woman turned, her familiar emerald eyes brightening. Her delicate features and light-blonde pixie-cut made her look even younger than her twenty-something years. "I need a canvas and some acrylics."

Moving behind the counter to the rack of small paint tubes against the wall, Erica gestured to her wares. "What size were you after? I have the acrylics in two ounces all the way up to sixty-four"—her hand waved toward the shelving on her left—"and the canvases come in square, rectangular—our smallest being the four-by-four inch. I think the biggest I have left in-store is a thirty-six-by-forty-eight, but I can always order in larger, even smaller if you'd prefer."

"Do you have the biggest canvas nearby? I'd like to check it over first, see if it's big enough."

Erica nodded. "In the storeroom, out the back." She looked closely at the young woman, noting a familiarity. "You work down the road, don't you? At Forrest's Organics, the fresh produce store? It's … Lauren, isn't it?"

The blonde woman grinned. "Yes, Lauren Perry. We've crossed paths a couple of times. You used to come into the store all the time a few years back."

"Yeah. When I first came to town, I started on a fitness kick. I was only buying organic, eating fruit and veggies, trying to keep up with the local health fanatics. It didn't last long though. I couldn't live without pizza and chocolate … or wine. Out of everything from back then, yoga is the only thing I've stuck to."

Lauren's eyes lit up. "Did you know we have organic chocolate and wine in-store? Even organic, nonalcoholic wine."

"Trying to save me from the dark side, are you?" Erica chuckled.

As she shrugged, Lauren's smile remained sweet and kind.

With another laugh, Erica motioned for Lauren to wait. "I'll be back in a moment with the canvas."

She headed for an open doorway to her right, flicking on a light switch inside the narrow room as she entered. Labeled brown cardboard boxes were stacked against the wall nearest the entrance, while tall, static shelving, full of inventory, hugged the parallel walls, tapering the room even tighter. At the very back, plastic-wrapped canvases of varying sizes rested alongside each other. Reaching them, Erica dug around, propping some aside to get access to the bigger ones.

Distracted by thoughts of her class, of completing the landscape painting, Erica moved a little faster. Once she'd made enough space to retrieve the largest canvas, she grabbed the thick frame and hauled the huge item up and out from the wall. Careful to clear the others she'd stacked beside it, she spun around but connected with the shelving structure to her right. Although it was bolted to the floor, it shook slightly, and she heard a couple of large *thuds* against the wooden floorboards.

She growled her displeasure and mentally scolded herself for attempting to move the gigantic item, instead of just taking Lauren into the storeroom to inspect it.

Sighing, Erica lowered the monstrosity to get a better look at the obstructions in front of her. She'd recently received an order of gesso—a white mixture used to prime the canvas before painting—and had restocked the shelf until the front two tubs sat slightly over the edge. Now those round containers were on the floor beyond her left foot—one on its side and one on its lid.

At least nothing breakable had fallen. Lifting the huge canvas higher again and holding it to her right, Erica stepped over the first obstacle. When she lifted her left foot over the second, the sound of footsteps entering the room had her gaze drifting upward.

Lauren let out a high-pitched squeak. "Are you okay?"

Erica nodded as her foot came down and clipped the edge of the circular tub. The container rolled, taking her heel with it, and she raised the canvas in the air struggling for balance. A garbled sound—part squeal, part yip—left her lips as she hit the floor hard on her right knee. Her bare skin skidded along the coarse wooden floorboards as her foot continued its ride. A split-second passed, something Erica experienced in slow-motion, and the tub popped free of her ankle before skittering across to the doorway. In her desperation for stability, she lowered the canvas and smacked herself in the face. When the ordeal was finally over, she was stretched across the floor, one leg in front, one behind, feeling sore, stupid, and sorry for herself, but so grateful her love of yoga had saved her from pulling a hamstring or breaking bone.

"Oh my God!" Lauren ran over to her. "Did I do that?"

Lowering the canvas to the floor, Erica rested it alongside the static shelves beside her. She brushed a loose lock of dark hair from her eyes before taking Lauren's outstretched hand.

"No. No." Erica shook her head, feeling everything ache as she stood. "Just me. My bad luck, really. I can be clumsy."

The *thudding* of more footsteps drew her attention to the storeroom's entry as she released Lauren's hand and brushed her own on her apron.

"What's happened?" Jocelyn's announcement was audible before she'd even entered.

When she came into view, her freckled cheeks were pinker than usual and her curly red-hair was gathering a frizz from her briskness. Erica smiled at her reassuringly as she adjusted the chocolate-brown bun atop her own head.

"Nothing to see here, Jocelyn. I had a little trip but survived the journey." She gestured at the large canvas, which was now sporting a slight indentation from where her nose had bashed into it. "Not sure I can say the same thing about the canvas."

"Oh, it's fine," Lauren said quickly, waving Erica's comment away with a flick of her wrist. "It's perfect. I'll take it."

Erica frowned. "It's damaged stock now. I can order in another."

Lauren shook her head. "It'll do, really."

As Erica opened her mouth to argue the point further, Jocelyn interrupted.

"Ladies!" It was almost a shriek.

"What?" Erica noticed the horror in the older woman's eyes and followed the direction of Jocelyn's outstretched index finger.

It was aimed at Erica's knee, the one that had dragged along the rough floorboards as she'd skidded ungracefully into the splits. There had been a slight stinging sensation, a constant ache, but Erica hadn't realized the damage she'd inflicted upon herself until now. Dark, garnet-red blood was thick in the grooves of the mutilated skin, while congealed snail-trails of scarlet crept down her shin.

Although the pain was distracting, she noticed it was only a flesh wound and bound to be a minor one once she'd had the time to clean it up.

"Oh dear." Lauren gasped.

"I'll call an ambulance." The concern in Jocelyn's tone was enough to have both of the younger women looking up at her again.

"No, Jocelyn—" Erica reached out in an effort to stop her, but the ginger-haired woman had already retreated inside the main room of the shop.

Fighting back the urge to limp, Erica hurried after her. She found her at the display counter, the cordless phone to her ear.

"Put the phone down." It was an order, said with only the slightest hint of menace.

Just the thought of having to explain herself to a pair of highly-skilled paramedics if Jocelyn was successful, was enough to have dread sitting heavily in Erica's stomach. She could already imagine their looks of displeasure.

Yes, sir. … It's just a skinned knee, sir. … Yes, I understand what an emergency is. … Yes, I know I'm taking your services away from someone who really needs your help, but you see, my friend here, she called you.

"Jocelyn." She offered her another warning.

"Don't use that tone with me, Erica."

She lifted her own dark eyebrow in challenge. "I am not going to the hospital over a scraped knee."

Jocelyn's eyes narrowed. "You're such a stubborn young woman."

Erica took that as a compliment, but then noticed the older woman's expression change, her gaze flickering across the shop as though concentrating on something only she was privy to.

"Yes. We need an ambulance."

Erica tried to snatch the phone away from Jocelyn's ear. "No, we don't."

"What's going on in here?" A male voice interrupted the jostle of hands.

Both of them glanced along the wall of open shelving, noticing the interest from those still seated in the classroom on the other side, before seeing Hamish striding over to them, his usually jolly countenance now full of concern.

Erica looked back at Jocelyn, giving her an opportunity to explain, but as the milliseconds passed, the attractive older woman's gray-green eyes became even more defiant.

Erica placed her hands on her hips. "Okay, what do you want?"

Jocelyn grinned smugly and covered the mouthpiece. "You don't want an ambulance, don't want to go to the hospital, fine. Then you let me take you to the doctor. I know what you're like, Erica. You'll patch this up yourself and wait for it to get infected before you even consider going to see a professional."

"I will n—" Erica would have finished her retort had Jocelyn not removed her hand from the bottom of the phone and dared her to continue with that twinkle in her eye. "Fine." It was said through gritted teeth. "I'll go to the doctor. Now, hang up and let them help someone who needs it."

The new doctor in town is attracting some attention, especially of the female persuasion, but art teacher, Erica Townsend is blissfully unaware until she ends up injured and in his office. Too bad she'd vowed to resist love—that traitorous emotion, the destroyer of lives—after numerous failed relationships. Something about Matt, about their electrifying connection has her wondering if he might just be…the one.

Dr. Matthew Garrick is tired of playing wing-man for his best friend. It isn't that he wishes to look for love, rather the opposite. But the eagerness of some of the single women in their small country town unnerves him. That is, until a certain stunning brunette appears in the waiting room of his medical practice. Her touch sparks something deep inside him, jolting his heart into a new rhythm and Matt makes it his mission to win's Erica love. Can he convince her to take a risk on him and what they share together?

As the good doctor strives to show Erica that love doesn't have to come at a price, his dangerous secret admirer threatens to prove otherwise.

Whoever said love wasn't dangerous?

Available where books are sold.

ABOUT THE AUTHOR

Tammy Mannersly is an Australian author based in Brisbane, Queensland. She loves writing romance, has a fondness for animals, is crazy about movies and enjoys a great Happily Ever After. Her passion for writing started from a very young age and led her to complete a Bachelor Degree in Creative Industries majoring in Creative Writing at Queensland University of Technology.

You can find out more information about Tammy and her work on her website: www.tammymannersly.com or by visiting:

Facebook: https://www.facebook.com/tammymannersly

Goodreads: https://www.goodreads.com/author/show/16935790.Tammy_Mannersly

Instagram: https://www.instagram.com/tammymannersly/

Twitter: https://twitter.com/TammyMannersly